Dave Darrin on the

Dave Darrin on the Asiatic Station

by H. Irving Hancock

CHAPTER I—TWO STRANGERS OF MANILA

"I am delighted to have had the privilege of meeting you, Miss Chapin," said Ensign Dave Darrin, lifting his uniform cap and bowing low at the end of the brief conversation. "And my thanks to you, Captain Chapin, for having afforded us the great pleasure."

Ensign Dan Dalzell, U. S. Navy, delivered himself in similar fashion.

The two young naval officers turned and were about to resume their stroll over the *Punta de España*, or Spanish bridge, which, crossing the Pasig River, separates Old Manila from New.

Just as suddenly, however, the pair checked their progress, to stare across the bridge.

On the opposite side, leaning against the rail, stood a Chinaman in rather rich apparel, with a decidedly sinister cast of countenance.

"Why is Old 'Burnt-face' staring so hard after Miss Chapin and her brother?" muttered Dalzell.

"I'm blessed if I know," returned Dave Darrin. "I've a good mind to cross over and put your question to the Chinaman."

"I've a greater mind to throw him into the Pasig," growled Dalzell. "I'm not strong on race lines or color, but I don't believe that any yellow man has a right to glare like that at an American girl."

Dalzell took a step forward, as though to cross the bridge, but Darrin promptly caught his wrist.

"Don't do anything rash, Danny Grin," urged Dave. "Throwing a Chinaman into a river isn't approved by the American government that has been set up in these islands."

"Then perhaps I'd better not hoist him over the bridge rail and let him drop into the water," Dan conceded. "But I believe that I will cross over and have a look at him."

"Not a bad idea, and certainly not against the law," nodded Ensign Darrin. "Let us follow the Chapins a little way, cross the road, and then come down on the other side so as to meet Mr. Burnt-face face to face."

The nickname that the American pair had given the yellow man was due to a patch of purple skin, of considerable area, under the yellow man's right eye. Had that patch been absent, undoubtedly the Chinaman would not have appeared so sinister.

"Odd that a fine girl like Miss Chapin should want to waste her life serving as a missionary in China, isn't it?" asked Dan.

"I wouldn't call it wasting her life," Darrin returned. "Neither, you may be sure, does Miss Chapin herself so consider it. To her way of thinking, she is devoting her life to one of the noblest ideals that can animate the human mind."

"I wouldn't mind so much if she were like the average girl," Dan rambled on, rather vaguely. "But for a stunner like Miss Chapin—such a dainty little piece of exquisite womanhood—"

"Oh," laughed Dave. "Then it isn't her services that you begrudge the natives of China, but her good looks."

"Well, anyway," Danny Grin continued rather testily, "I'll wager that Chapin doesn't fully approve of what his sister is doing."

Captain Chapin was serving in one of the infantry regiments of the Army line at Manila. Being stationed in the city, Chapin had the good fortune to have his family, consisting of his mother, wife and two young children, located in a cottage over in Ermita, just beyond the massive stone walls of Old Manila. Miss Lucy Chapin was visiting her brother on her way to China, where a missionary post awaited her. Knowing Captain Chapin from the stirring days of service in Mexico, the two young naval officers, on meeting him here in Manila, the "Paris of the East," had been presented to that charming young woman.

Crossing the roadway near the Old Manila end of the bridge, Dave and Dan strolled back. In the meantime "Burnt-face," as Dan had named him, had turned and was heading toward the Escolta, the Broadway of New Manila.

Both young officers wore the white service uniform of the tropics. Here and there a soldier or sailor, in passing, brought his hand to his cap in smart salute, a courtesy which both officers, in every instance, returned.

"That's our fellow," whispered Darrin, slowing down his step.

"Burnt-face," a man of somewhere near forty, if it be possible to judge a Chinaman's age, kept on his way at a pace neither hurried nor slow. Three different times parties of Chinese coolies passed him. On perceiving "Burnt-face" they lowered their eyes to the ground in passing.

Near the end of the bridge two much better dressed Chinamen passed the yellow man whom the young naval officers were now following. This pair made deferential bows, then moved slightly aside in order not to compel "Burnt-face" to step out of his own course.

"Our man is a chap of some importance," murmured Darrin.

"He may be—to a Chinaman!" grunted Danny Grin.

Reaching the end of the bridge, the Chinaman paused, then started to cross the street as if to go to the famous Café de Paris.

Honk! honk! A touring car, going at about twelve miles an hour, rolled down out of the nearby Escolta, heading for the bridge. With an agile bound "Burnt-face" leaped back to the sidewalk.

"Look at the scowl he's sending after that car," whispered Dalzell.

"His lips are moving, too," returned Darrin, quietly observant. "If it weren't for the look on his face I should say that our chap was praying."

"In his case," muttered Dalzell, "he's more likely cursing."

"But say," Dave went on. "Just observe how 'Burnt-face' continues to glare after that car."

"Can he have anything against the people in the car?" Dan wondered.

"It is more likely that his hatred is directed against the car itself," Darrin replied.

"But why should he hate a mere assemblage of mechanical units?" Dan demanded.

"I suppose that, being a Chinaman, he regards an automobile as the work of the Evil One," Dave smiled. "Your real, old-fashioned Chinaman isn't strong for new-fangled ideas. In some parts of China the appearance of an automobile, even to-day, would rouse a mob to wild fury."

"Queer old place, China!" uttered Dalzell.

"Since we're waiting orders to go to China, you'll soon know," Dave rejoined.

"I don't believe I shall like China," Dan declared prophetically.

Now that the road was clear, "Burnt-face" crossed the street. He did not go to the Café de Paris, but stepped up in front of a drug store, where he halted and turned around.

In passing, Dave and Dan managed, without staring, to get a good look at the yellow face. In addition to the purple mark under the right eye, "Burnt-face," with his lips parted, displayed one incisor tooth, the lower end of which had been broken off. At the left side of his chin was a mark such as might have been made by a knife or a bullet.

"He's an ugly-looking customer," Dan muttered, when he and his chum had passed a few yards beyond the drug store.

"That face carries a history," guessed Darrin. "Nor do I believe that it is a very savory history."

"I believe that the only real pirates left in the world," observed Dan, "are the Black Flags that every now and then infest Chinese waters. I wonder if 'Burnt-face' were ever apprenticed to the Black Flags."

"Don't talk about him any more," murmured Dave, after a backward glance. "The Chinaman is now returning our late courtesies by following *us*."

Attracted by the window display of a shop that dealt in Hindu curios, the two young naval officers went inside.

"I want to buy something pretty with which to surprise Belle," Dave explained, as the chums roamed through the shop, inspecting the hundreds of quaint and artistic articles offered for sale.

"You expect her to reach Manila the 26th of the month, don't you?" Dan asked.

"The 16th," Darrin corrected his chum.

"Due here in eleven days?" cried Dalzell, sharing his comrade's pleasure in the thought. "My, Dave, you're a very lucky young man!"

"It seems ages since I said good-bye to Belle," Dave went on musingly. "Dan, it almost seems as if I had not seen my wife since she and I were high school sweethearts."

"I can take my oath that you've seen her more recently than that," laughed Dan. "Yet I know that it must seem a long while between your meetings."

A Hindu salesman, wearing European clothes, topped by a real Hindu turban, now approached them.

"Something really nice for a lady," Dave nodded.

"Pardon, excellency," replied the Hindu, with a low bow. "Is the lady—ah—young?"

"Yes," assented Ensign Darrin.

"May I—ah—inquire whether the young lady be—ah—wife, sweetheart, or sister?" suggested the Hindu, with a second bow that was lower than the first.

"Why do you need to know that?" demanded Dave, frowning slightly. "She's the finest girl on earth. Isn't that enough for you to know?"

"Then," declared the Hindu imperturbably, "she is your sweetheart, and in that case I am certain that I know exactly what to show you."

"Oh, you do?" grimaced Ensign Darrin. "Then trot out the best you have."

"Will your excellency condescend to step this way?" proposed the Hindu, with the lowest bow yet. "I shall exert myself to show you the very finest that we have suitable for distinguished presentation to a sweetheart."

Down to a vault, at the rear of the shop, the salesman led the way. Opening the vault door he nimbly slipped out two trays of exquisite yet eccentric Hindu jewelry.

"Now, let the excellency gloat over these," begged the salesman, throwing out a bewildering array of rings, brooches, amulets, bracelets, neck chains and the like, set in a dazzling array of precious and semi-precious gems.

"How much is this chain?" asked Dave, picking up one of beautiful workmanship.

"The price of that, excellency, is twelve hundred dollars, but as a very special favor to an officer in the Service I will allow it to go out of the store at eleven hundred."

Sighing, Dave laid the chain down.

"It is not fine enough, I know, excellency," glowed the salesman. "Now, look at this chain. Is it not handsomer?"

"Yes," Dave admitted.

"This chain, excellency, is a wonderful bargain at fifteen hundred dollars."

Dave sighed, but declined to examine the chain.

"Even if you had the money with you," remarked Danny Grin, "your wife would hardly think you displayed good judgment in spending almost a year's salary to buy her a chain."

"Oh, it is for your wife?" exclaimed the Hindu, in an almost shocked voice.

"Yes," Dave assented.

"Oh, in that case, excellency—"

With incredibly rapid movements the Hindu put the articles back into the two drawers, shoved them into the vault and closed the door.

"Here you are, excellency!" cried the Oriental, springing to a near-by counter. "Here is a chain of considerable beauty, and it costs but six dollars."

Giving a momentary gasp, Darrin eyed the fellow, then suddenly reached over and took him in a tight collar grip.

"What do you mean, Mr. Insolence?" Darrin demanded sternly. "Do you wish to insinuate that a sweetheart calls for a handsome gift, but that anything is good enough for a wife?"

"Er—ah—in *my* country, excellency, when one buys for a sweetheart it is one thing. When he buys for a wife—"

"Then thank goodness that my country isn't your country," uttered Ensign Darrin disgustedly, while Danny Grin implored:

"Before you let him go, Davy, turn him around this way so that I may register at least one kick!"

But Darrin suddenly released the rather frightened fellow, saying crisply:

"Show me some pieces of jewelry at prices around fifty dollars."

At first the salesman displayed several pieces for which he asked from seventy-five to a hundred dollars.

"You're wasting my time, but I won't waste yours," Dave suddenly broke in, turning away.

"Wait a moment, excellency. Do you realize, excellency, that you have not, in any instance, attempted to bargain with me?"

"Do you mean that you expect me to work you down to a lower price?" asked Ensign Dalzell, lowering his voice.

"It is customary to bargain, excellency," replied the Hindu, with a bow, though not so low as he had displayed at first.

"I'm not going to bargain with you," Dave declared quietly. "At any price you name for an article I shall either accept the price, and pay it, or else refuse further to consider that article. And don't waste any more of my time. At the first sign of it I shall quit your store and not enter it again."

Still the Hindu tried high prices for a while, then suddenly held up a necklace set with small, beautiful bits of jade.

"Eighty dollars," he exclaimed.

"Mex?" broke in Dan quickly.

"Of course, excellency," confirmed the Hindu.

"See here, David, little giant," Danny Grin rattled on, "we've been going it a bit blind. We've been thinking of gold, or American dollars, while this man has been talking on the basis of the Mexican silver dollar."

In the Philippine Islands the Mexican dollar is still the basis of currency. As this dollar is worth less than half of that amount in gold, the price charged by the Hindu, translated into American money, amounted to less than forty dollars.

"I'll take it," Dave announced, after a keen inspection of the necklace.

Payment was made, and the necklace was placed in a box so small that Ensign Darrin was easily able to drop it into one of his pockets.

From the curb outside a pair of glittering, bead-like eyes had peered into the gloom of the store.

Dave and Dan left the curio shop, the former feeling happier at thought of the pleasant surprise secured for Belle.

Further up the Escolta there now appeared a somewhat Americanized Chinese youth, of perhaps sixteen years, who soon started indolently on the trail of the strolling naval officers.

"Where now?" inquired Danny Grin.

"Have you anything that you wish to do ashore?" Dave asked.

"Nothing."

"Neither have I, so suppose we go down to the office of the Captain of the Port. Our launch should be in soon."

"Suits me," nodded Dan.

These two young officers are the same Dave and Dan whose fortunes our readers have followed through many volumes full of exciting adventures and strange incidents.

Our readers first met them in the pages of the "Grammar School Boys Series," in which Darrin and Dalzell appeared as members of that now famous group of six schoolboys who were collectively known as Dick & Co., taking that name from their leader, Dick Prescott. Their adventures are further to be found in the High School Boys Series, and in the High School Vacation Series.

At the end of high school days Dick Prescott and Greg Holmes went to the United States Military Academy at West Point. What there befell the two cadets is set forth in the pages of the West Point Series. The professional careers of Tom Reade and Harry Hazelton, once also of Dick & Co., are to be found in the exciting volumes of the Young Engineers Series. Dave Darrin and Dan Dalzell, as all our readers are aware, were appointed midshipmen at the United States Naval Academy at Annapolis, and their lives in that famous training school are splendidly depicted in the Annapolis Series.

The present series, as our readers know, depicts the life of Dave and Dan at sea as young officers. The first volume, "Dave Darrin at Vera Cruz," deals with the famous events suggested by the title. In the second volume, "Dave Darrin on Mediterranean Service," is told what befell our young friends in their efforts to frustrate an international plot of possibly grave consequence to this country. The third volume, "Dave Darrin's South American Cruise," which our readers have lately read, deals with the adventures of the two young naval officers in foiling the outrageous plots of a South American ex-dictator, scheming to get back into power. And now, at last, we find Dave and Dan on the Asiatic Station.

Hardly had the naval officers turned out of the Escolta, at the water front, when Dan noticed that the sidewalk held at least fifty Chinese.

"This is the greatest of American cities, as far as Chinese population goes," smiled Dave. "Manila never has less than a hundred thousand Chinese residents."

Out in the road stood a solitary member of the Chinese population. At a signal from the youth behind the naval officers, he said a few words in guttural undertone.

Quickly the Chinese came together, jabbering and crowding the sidewalk.

"Gangway!" cried Danny Grin, as he and Dave found themselves pressing through the yellow throng.

Slowly, rather indifferently, the Chinese made way for the two naval officers to step through the crowd. Had Dave and Dan gone out into the road to get around this crowd it would have been at the expense of their dignity in a city where no white man is supposed to allow coolies to block his way.

"Gangway!" roared Dalzell.

The Americanized Chinese boy was now close beside the naval officers. A small, skinny yellow hand reached out.

"I'm sure Belle will be delighted with that necklace," Dave murmured to himself.

Alas! That jewel box no longer rested in his pocket, for the yellow boy with the bead-like eyes, at that very instant, had filched the little package. Nor did the picking of the white men's pockets cease at that point.

8

Once through the throng, the two young ensigns were not long in reaching the building in which are situated the offices of the Captain of the Port. It is opposite this building, on the bank of the Pasig River, where launches from naval vessels and army transports come in and tie up.

"Launch not in," announced Danny Grin.

"We'll have some minutes to wait," Dave answered. "Let's go over there and get a soda."

"Over there" referred to a little white one-story building, in which plain soda and similar beverages were sold.

Dave and Dan stepped inside, calling for soda water and drinking thirstily.

"Tastes good," muttered Dan. "Let's have another."

So the second soda was ordered, and was finished more slowly. Then Darrin reached into one of his pockets. Soon he explored another pocket.

"Why, that's queer!" muttered Dave, aloud. "I thought my money—"

"Never mind your money, chum," interrupted Dan Dalzell. "I'll pay for—"

A few seconds later Dan's expression changed to one of great amazement.

"Why, where *is* my money?" he gasped.

"Don't look for it," returned Dave. "I don't believe you'll find it. For myself, my pockets have been completely cleaned out. I haven't even the necklace that I bought for Belle."

"Look here!" uttered Danny Grin, his lower jaw dropping low, indeed. "Have we been robbed? Have our pockets been gone through just as if we were a pair of rubes?"

"Our pockets have been picked all right," Darrin assented, with a smile.

"Then it was done while we were in that Chinese sidewalk mob!" said Dan, quivering with rage. "Just wait until I overhaul 'em, and—"

Dan sprang outside. His good intentions, however, came to naught, for the crowd of Chinese had disappeared.

"It's a good joke on us," grinned Dave, though not very mirthfully.

"Oh, is it?" flashed back Danny Grin. "Then enjoy yourself! Laugh as heartily as you can. But I've been touched for two hundred and forty dollars. How much did you lose?"

"A hundred and sixty dollars, and the necklace," confessed Darrin.

"Say," muttered Ensign Dalzell, another strange look coming into his face as he made another discovery. "I wish I could find those yellow-faced thieves."

"Why?"

"They overlooked something," almost exploded Dalzell. "They didn't get my watch. It seems to me that it would be no more than honest to run after them and hand them that, also."

Dan held up his gold watch.

"They left my watch in my clothes, too," nodded Dave.

"I wonder why?" murmured Dalzell.

"Over four hundred dollars, from the two of us," muttered Dave, staring grimly up the road. "Not a bad two minutes' work for some one."

"It would make me feel more kindly to the poor fellow if only he'd come back and take my watch and chain," declared Danny Grin. "I hate to see a poor thief overlook anything of value."

"I was wondering," Dave continued, "whether it would do any good to complain to the police. On second thought, I believe I shall write the chief of police after I go aboard ship. If there's a regular gang working this part of Manila, then the police ought to know it, but I've no idea that the police would be able to get our money back."

"That money has been under cover for some minutes," rejoined Dalzell. "If you've any loose change you might settle our bill here."

"I haven't a cent," Darrin confessed.

But the proprietor of the little shop begged the young gentlemen to forget the little bit of small change that they owed him. This both Dan and Dave refused to do, promising to pay him the next time they came ashore.

No sooner did they step outside than they were confronted by a well-dressed, tall young man under thirty.

"I hope you'll pardon me," said this stranger, with a rather decided English accent, "but I couldn't possibly help overhearing your conversation inside. For that reason I know that you have had the misfortune to be robbed of your money by Chinese thieves. Now—no offense intended, I assure you—could I be of any manner of use to you? Pembroke is my name, you know; Pembroke of Heathshire, England. I'm on my way around the world. Now, if between one gentlemen and two others, you know, I could be of any—"

The Englishman paused, as if embarrassed; it was plain that he was trying to offer a loan of money.

"I think I understand you, Mr. Pembroke," Ensign Darrin replied, with a grateful smile. "It is extremely kind in you, but the robbery has left us embarrassed only for a moment. Both of us have funds deposited with the paymaster on board ship, and after we go aboard it is only a matter of asking for what we need."

"You're not annoyed, I trust," murmured Pembroke apologetically.

"No; profoundly glad to find such faith in human nature as you have displayed," smiled Ensign Darrin.

"Oh, I don't trust the whole blooming human race," declared Mr. Pembroke gravely. "I'm not such a simpleton as that. But I know that good old Uncle Sam's officers are gentlemen, and between gentlemen, you know, there is and should be a lot of jolly confidence."

In the easiest way in the world, Mr. Pembroke was now sauntering along with the two young Americans.

"Do you know much about the Chinese?" Dave inquired.

"Not enough to make me like 'em a precious lot," replied Pembroke.

"I wish I could understand their lingo," muttered Dalzell.

"And I'm positively proud that I don't!" glowed Mr. Pembroke.

They had halted at the water's edge, now, Dan turning his eyes in the direction of the breakwater to see if he could make out the launch for which he and his chum waited.

10

"Here comes a fuzzy-fuzzy boat," announced Dalzell, at last. "But it's not ours. Just as it happens, the craft is a Frenchman."

Pembroke cast a glance at the approaching launch, then went on chatting with Darrin.

Presently the launch ran in alongside, a middle-aged French officer stepping up on the jetty not fifty feet from where Dave and his companions stood.

The Frenchman started rather visibly when his gaze rested on Pembroke. Dave noticed that. And Pembroke saw the Frenchman, for one fleeting instant. Then the Englishman turned his back squarely, while the French naval officer, holding himself very erect, and with a frown on his face, returned the courteous salute of the young American officers.

"Do you know that gentleman, Mr. Pembroke?" Dave asked quietly.

"Never saw him before," declared Mr. Pembroke coldly.

"That's odd," reflected Dave. "If faces are books, and if glances may be read, I should have said that the Frenchman didn't like our very courteous Englishman."

The French officer was now passing out of sight.

"I see our launch," called out Danny Grin.

"I say, Mr. Darrin, by the way," spoke up the Englishman, "what is your ship?"

"The gunboat 'Castoga'," Darrin answered.

"Then, if you don't mind, I'm going to do myself the honor, some afternoon in the near future, of going out to your ship and calling on you. I find it very dull here in Manila, you know, and I shall be glad to see more of you both."

"We shall undoubtedly meet at one of the clubs ashore," Dave smiled back steadily into the other's eyes. "In that case, I'll try to introduce you to our commanding officer, and I've no doubt that he'll be glad to extend you a cordial invitation to come aboard."

A few moments later the launch from the "Castoga" came gliding in at the jetty. Dave and Dan extended their hands to Mr. Pembroke, then stepped aboard the launch, leaving the Englishman to turn away.

Nor had he more than turned his back when Pembroke allowed a very distinct frown to gather on his face.

In front of the office of the Captain of the Port, Pembroke came face to face with the same French naval officer. The two men regarded each other stolidly and passed on without speaking.

CHAPTER II—THE TRAGEDY OF THE BAY

"Why did you turn the Englishman down so hard?" asked Danny Grin, as he and Dave sat at the stern of the launch that sped down the river and then out to the naval anchorage in the bay.

"I didn't," Darrin replied.

"You shut off his proposal to visit us on board."

"Dan, didn't you notice the look that French naval officer gave Pembroke?"

"No."

"Perhaps you noticed how stiffly the Frenchman stepped away after returning our salutes."

11

"I saw that," said Dan, "and wondered at it."

"I think the French officer was trying to flag to us an intimation that Pembroke isn't one who would pass inspection in naval circles."

"No?" gasped Danny Grin, looking genuinely astonished. "It never struck me that way. He had the appearance and the manners of a gentleman."

"So has many an international confidence man," Dave rejoined. "I don't know a blessed thing against Pembroke, and perhaps the Frenchman doesn't either. Unless I can find out something definite about the Englishman, I hardly care to be the one to introduce him to our little wardroom crowd."

"I see," nodded Dalzell thoughtfully. "You're right, Dave. One can't be too careful about his introductions, nor can one very well receive callers on board ship without making them known to the other wardroom fellows."

After the three battleships on which our young naval officers had served, the "Castoga" did seem small by comparison, although she was a gunboat of comfortable dimensions, with an ample wardroom for the number of officers carried, and with all the ordinary provisions for comfort afloat.

With a crew of one hundred and thirty sailors supplemented by a detachment of thirty marines; with a large enough crew in the engineer's department, and with nine officers, including a surgeon and a paymaster's clerk, in addition to three engineer officers, the "Castoga" carried a businesslike complement.

Lieutenant-Commander Tuthill was the commanding officer, with Lieutenant Warden as executive officer. The four watch officers were all ensigns.

After reporting their return to the officer of the deck, Dave and Dan went promptly to their quarters. Here, after bathing, they dressed for dinner, which was due to be served in less than half an hour.

At table, later, Dave told the tale of the robbery that afternoon. Dan added the tale of their meeting with Pembroke, and of that Englishman's offer to loan them money.

"What kind of fellow is that Pembroke?" asked Lieutenant Warden.

Dave described the Englishman, adding, questioningly:

"Do you know him, sir, or know of him?"

"No," replied Mr. Warden.

"I thought that Pembroke must be known to a French naval officer who passed us," continued Darrin, and related that incident, too.

"The Frenchman's shrug was nothing against the Englishman," remarked Lieutenant Warden. "It might have been merely instinctive aversion, or it might mean merely that the Frenchman and the Englishman had a dispute in the past, at this or some other port. Otherwise it would be odd indeed to see a Frenchman turn the cold shoulder on an Englishman when their countrymen are standing shoulder to shoulder on the long battle lines in Europe."

"Surely, if the French officer knew Pembroke to be a gentleman, he would have rushed up and gripped Pembroke's hand just out of a sentimental feeling for the strong bonds of friendship between France and England in these dark days in Europe," nodded Dan understandingly.

"Pembroke wanted to come on board, sir," Ensign Darrin went on, "but I couldn't help feeling that, before inviting him, I would like to know more about him."

"Caution of that sort is never amiss," nodded the executive officer thoughtfully. "By the way, you don't imagine that there could have been any connection between the thieving Chinese and Mr. Pembroke, do you?"

"Why, I hadn't thought of it in that way," Ensign Darrin confessed. "There isn't usually, is there, much connection between a thief who robs you and a man who offers to lend you a little money?"

"There might be easily," said Mr. Warden.

"Our last half hour on shore was a puzzle altogether," Dave went on, after a short pause. "First, we followed that burnt-face Chinaman. Then we ran into a crowd of Chinese who cleaned out our pockets of everything but our watches. And then we met Pembroke, at whom the French officer turned up his nose. I am now actually beginning to wonder if 'Burnt-face,' the thieves and Pembroke may not all be links in a chain of mystery."

"At least Pembroke doesn't speak or understand the Chinese language," Dalzell broke in.

"He *said* he didn't," Dave returned. "However, if Pembroke is not a gentleman and a straightforward fellow, it is as easy to believe that he lied as that he spoke the truth."

"Don't bother any more about it," advised Ensign Hale bluffly. "The money is gone. As to the rest of the story, it isn't worth puzzling your heads over. Your adventure was all grossly material. No such things as mysteries or romances are left in the world—nothing but work."

"Nevertheless," smiled Ensign Darrin seriously, "I shall continue to admit myself puzzled until I have succeeded in gathering certain information that I really wish."

"What kind of information?" asked Hale.

"For instance, I want to know if 'Burnt-face' has any connection with the yellow boys who went through our pockets."

"I think that at least half likely," replied Ensign Hale gravely.

"And then, next, I want to know," Darrin went on, "if there is any connection between 'Burnt-face' and Pembroke."

"That is much less likely," answered Hale.

"Last of all, if Pembroke is in the least shady, I'd like to know something definite about him," wound up Ensign Dave.

"Go to the Frenchman for that," advised Hale.

"Thank you; I believe I shall."

"But what does it matter, Darrin," asked Lieutenant Warden, "whether Pembroke is all right, or not? You turned him aside from visiting this craft, so what does it matter whether the fellow is a gentleman or the reverse?"

"Because," replied Dave Darrin, so solemnly that some of his brother officers stared, "I have a premonition that I'm going to meet Pembroke again, and under conditions where I shall be glad to know something definite about the fellow."

At eight bells in the evening Ensign Dalzell went on duty as officer of the deck. Darrin, aroused in season from a nap, took over the watch at midnight.

"Any orders?" asked Darrin of his chum.

"None, save the usual orders for the safety and security of the ship," Dalzell replied. Salutes were exchanged, and the former officer of the deck hurried to his quarters.

A marine sentry paced aft, another forward. Six sailormen, including two petty officers, occupied their posts about the deck and on the bridge. Two or three of the engine-room crew were on watch below. The others on board slept, for the night was clear and the gunboat at anchorage half a mile out from the mouth of the Pasig River.

After the first tour of inspection to see that all was snug, Ensign Darrin leaned against the quarter rail, looking out over the water. By this time the sky had clouded somewhat, though the barometer remained stationary, showing that no atmospheric disturbances were to be looked for at present.

The night was so still that nothing but the discipline of trained habit prevented Ensign Darrin from nodding, then falling asleep.

Even as it was, his eyelids drooped almost to the closing point as he leaned there over the rail. But he was not asleep.

After some minutes Dave opened his eyes wider, straightened up and glanced out sharply over the water, on which objects were not now so clearly visible as they had been at midnight.

"That sounded like a paddle," Darrin told himself, then added, in a low voice: "Sentry!"

"Aye, aye, sir," replied the marine, in a low voice, at the same time giving the rifle salute.

"I thought I heard a boat approaching yonder. Keep your eye open for any kind of craft coming near."

"Aye, aye, sir!"

It was Ensign Darrin who discovered a small, outrigger canoe stealing forward in the night. Two seconds later the marine also reported it. Calling the nearest sailor to him, Dave gave him brief, whispered instructions which sent the young man slipping noiselessly forward.

"Shall I hail that craft, sir?" whispered the sentry, standing stiffly beside the young officer.

"Not yet," Dave rejoined. Both stood there, watching keenly. Few landsmen, on such a night, would have been able to make out so small a craft at such a distance. Those who follow the sea are trained to cat-like vision.

"Sentry," whispered Dave, "do you make out a second craft, following the first?"

"Just barely sir," replied the sentry, after a sharp look.

Unless the two small craft changed their courses speedily Darrin knew that he would have to hail them and warn them off. In these piping times of peace in the Philippines, there was nothing very suspicious in two boats coming close to a war vessel at anchor. Still, the two canoes could not be permitted to come up alongside without the occupants first giving an account of themselves.

14

"It looks like a race," Dave told himself, as he continued to watch intently. "Jove, I am tempted to believe that the second canoe is trying to overtake the leader. What can it—"

In the act of bawling an order forward, Ensign Dave Darrin felt his tongue hit the roof of his mouth. For, at this instant, the pursuing canoe ranged up alongside the first.

There was a dim flash of something, accompanied by a yell of unearthly terror.

"Light!" shouted Dave Darrin huskily.

"Aye, aye, sir."

In a twinkling, the narrow, dazzling beam of one of the forward searchlights shot over the water.

Within three seconds it had picked up the smaller of the canoes. To the watchers from the deck of the gunboat this canoe appeared to be empty.

Then the light shifted enough to pick up the second, larger canoe, now darting shoreward under the impetus of two powerful paddlers.

"Ahoy, there, shorebound boat!" yelled Ensign Darrin lustily. "Lay to and give an account of yourselves!"

The challenged canoe moved on so rapidly as to call for the constant shifting of the searchlight's beam.

"Lay to, there, or we fire!" bellowed Ensign Darrin over the rippling waters of Manila Bay.

But the canoe made no sign of halting.

"Sentry!"

"Aye, aye, sir."

"Take aim and hold it!"

"Aye, aye, sir."

Then again Dave challenged.

"Shorebound boat, third challenge! Lay to, instantly!"

No attention being paid by the two paddlers, Ensign Darrin now gave the sharp order:

"Fire!"

That bullet must have whistled uncomfortably close to the fleeing craft, for on the instant both paddlers rose in the canoe.

"Fire!" commanded Ensign Dave, the second time.

At the sound of the marine's shot both poised figures sprang overboard from the canoe.

"Shall I fire again, sir?" asked the marine, as the beam of the searchlight continued to play upon the waters where the divers had vanished.

"Not unless you see those men that jumped overboard from that canoe," replied Ensign Darrin.

Though the searchlight continued to flash further across the water, nothing was seen of the men from the canoe. Indeed, at the distance, the rippling waves might easily conceal a swimmer.

"Pass the word for the boatswain's mate!" Darrin ordered.

As that petty officer appeared, Darrin ordered him to turn out a boat crew and put one of the boats over the side.

15

"First investigate the nearer canoe, then the second. Bring them both in alongside. If you see any swimmers in the water, pursue and pick them up."

"Aye, aye, sir."

Still the searchlight continued to play over the waters. The "Castoga's" small boat ranged alongside the smaller outrigger canoe, and soon had it in tow with a line astern. A minute or two after the second canoe was picked up. A short search was made for swimmers, after which, on signal, the boatswain's mate turned and headed for the gunboat.

"Ship's boat ahoy!" Dave called, as the boat and its tows came near.

"Ahoy the deck, sir!"

"Are both canoes empty?" Darrin inquired.

"The first one isn't, sir," replied the boatswain's mate. "There's a dead Chinaman in it. Head almost cut off; sword work, I should say, sir."

"Bring both tows alongside," Dave ordered, with a shiver. "I will communicate with the police."

After ordering a wireless operator turned out, Ensign Darrin went over the side, down a sea-ladder, to the smaller of the outrigger canoes.

Huddled in a heap in the canoe, was a Chinaman who did not seem to be more than thirty years of age. His head, nearly severed from his body, had fallen forward until it hung close to the dead man's chest. It was only by turning the head that Ensign Darrin was able to see the face, on which there still lingered a look of terror.

"A Chinese tong-fight or a gang murder," Dave told himself, in keen disgust.

Then climbing up over the side he sent an orderly to summon the executive officer.

Less than three minutes later Lieutenant Warden, fully dressed, and wearing his sword, walked briskly out upon the quarter-deck.

The executive officer listened intently while Ensign Darrin made his report with conciseness.

"I'll take a look at the body," said Mr. Warden, and went down over the side. He came up again, horror written in every line of his face.

"A cowardly killing, Ensign Darrin," declared the executive officer. "Notify the Manila police by wireless."

"Aye, aye, sir."

"Call me again, if I am needed."

"Aye, aye, sir."

The instant Darrin had saluted and Mr. Warden had turned on his heel, Dave, under a light just inside the superstructure, wrote a few words which he signed in his official capacity as officer of the deck. This was sent forward to the waiting wireless operator, who sent the message to a military station on shore, whence the message was telephoned to police headquarters.

Within three minutes the wireless operator, ran aft, saluting, and reported:

"A police launch will put off immediately, and come out, sir."

Fifteen minutes later a motor launch, flying the police ensign, ranged up alongside the "Castoga." An American official, accompanied by four Filipino policemen, came on board.

16

Dave at once narrated what had happened, after which the American police official inspected both canoes and looked at the huddled yellow body.

"This will require investigation, sir," declared the police official. "I shall tow both canoes ashore, and then the force will get busy."

"Don't you wish to send a wireless ashore, urging the police to look out for two swimmers who are likely to attempt to land?" suggested Dave.

"An excellent idea," replied the police official, and wrote out a despatch which Ensign Darrin sent to the wireless operator forward.

After that the launch chugged away with the two canoes in tow.

Twenty minutes later a wireless message was received aboard the "Castoga," and immediately the operator brought it aft.

"Native Policeman Rafeta," Ensign Darrin read, "reports that a Chinese swimmer was observed, by him, to land. The Chinaman reported that his skiff had upset. Native policeman, not being suspicious, reports that he allowed swimmer to proceed on his way. Swimmer is to be identified by a fire-mark on the right cheek under eye."

"Burnt-face!" gasped Ensign Dave, recoiling slightly. "Then it seems that I was not quit of that fellow when I turned my back on him on the Escolta this afternoon. In what fiendish business can 'Burnt-face' be engaged?"

CHAPTER III—MR. PEMBROKE BREAKS IN

On the next day the Manilla police had little of interest to add to the account of the night tragedy on Manilla Bay.

Searching the city, and especially the Chinese quarters, the police had been unable to find any yellow man answering to the description of "Burnt-face."

Very likely many of the Chinese residents of the city knew the man who was sought, but Chinamen habitually mind their own business, even to the extent of withholding important information from the police. So within two or three days the chase was all but forgotten. The Chinese "tongs" are secret societies that commit killings in all parts of the globe where their people are to be found, and the death of an unknown Chinaman does not provoke the police anywhere to any great zeal in finding the slayer.

Then the "Castoga," which, for reasons known only to the higher naval authorities, had been anchored half a mile from the mouth of the Pasig, was ordered to new anchorage off the naval station at Cavite.

On board, the officers had ceased to speak of the strange Chinese tragedy of the night; Dave and Dan had well-nigh ceased to think about it.

One afternoon the French gunboat "Revanche" received visitors. Ensigns Darrin, Dalzell and Hale were requested to represent the "Castoga" and did so, going over in the launch.

On board the French boat they found a sprinkling of English and Japanese naval officers. There were also a few officers from the United States Army.

Our American friends were introduced to all present whom they had not previously known. Half an hour later Darrin was inspecting the "Revanche's" lifeboat equipment under the escort of Lieutenant Brun, of the French Navy, when a superior officer appeared on deck. It was the same officer who had appeared, on shore, to exhibit such marked disapproval of Mr. Pembroke.

"There's an officer over there to whom I wish you would introduce me," Dave said to the lieutenant.

"With great pleasure," replied Brun, "as soon as our turn comes. That is Commander Bertrand, commanding the 'Revanche.' All the gentlemen present will be introduced to him now."

"If you don't mind," Dave added, quickly, in French, "I shall be glad to wait until the last, as I should like to have a few words with your commander."

A group had gathered around Commander Bertrand, who, all smiles and good will, played the host to perfection.

At last Lieutenant Brun led Dave over to be introduced. The introduction accomplished, Brun moved away a short distance.

After the first few polite exchanges had been made on both sides, Dave asked:

"Would you object, sir, to telling me whether you know a Mr. Pembroke, an Englishman?"

"I know that it is a well-known English name," replied Commander Bertrand, "but personally I know no Englishman of that name."

"Do you remember seeing Mr. Dalzell and myself with a man in front of the office of the Captain of the Port a few days ago?"

"I recall having passed you," replied the Frenchman readily.

"That was Mr. Pembroke with whom we were talking."

"Was it?" inquired the Frenchman politely, as he raised his eyebrows. "Then perhaps I was in error. I felt that I had seen the man before, but at that time his name was Rogers."

"May I inquire, sir, if you know this man Rogers?"

Commander Bertrand shrugged his shoulders slightly as he asked:

"Is he a friend of yours, Monsieur Darrin?"

"No; but he had presented himself to Mr. Dalzell and me, and then had offered to do us a service."

"I do not believe that I would trust him," replied the Frenchman. "I cannot say, positively, that Monsieur Rogers and Monsieur Pembroke are one and the same man, but this I can assure you—that Monsieur Rogers is far from being an honest man."

Further than that the French officer seemed disinclined to discuss the subject. After a brief chat on other topics Dave thanked the French Commander courteously and moved away. In less than two minutes, however, Dave found a chance to impart this information briefly to Danny Grin.

"Pembroke looks like a good one to dodge," declared Ensign Dalzell.

"I don't know," returned Dave Darrin. "It all hinges on whether he is really the chap who once called himself Rogers. Commander Bertrand declined to be positive that they are one and the same, though for himself, he seems to believe it. However, we are not likely to see Pembroke again. He has made no effort to force himself upon us."

Not long after that the launch called, and the "Castoga's" visiting officers started to return to their own craft.

"There is some one waving to us," declared Dave, staring across the water at the occupants of a small motor boat.

"Why, it looks like Captain Chapin," returned Dalzell.

"It *is* Chapin, and that is his sister with him," returned Dave. "See, she is standing up in the bow to wave her handkerchief to us."

"Chapin ought not to allow her to stand up in the bow of such a narrow craft," said Danny Grin. "It's a risky pose for any one but a veteran sailor. It's dangerous. She—"

"By Jove!" burst from Darrin. "There she goes—overboard!"

For a rolling wave, catching the small motor boat under the bow, had rocked the little craft.

Miss Chapin was seen to stagger wildly and then plunge overboard.

"They've stopped!" cried Dan. "She doesn't come up, either!"

"Boatswain's mate!" rang out Ensign Darrin's voice sharply to the naval launch alongside. "Put over there at once. Run astern of the motor boat's position."

"Aye, aye, sir," and the naval launch swung briskly around.

"I beg your pardon, Hale, for forgetting that you are ranking officer here," Dave apologized, keeping his gaze out over the water.

"There's no apology needed," returned Ensign Hale. "Our only need is to reach the spot as quickly as possible."

The motor boat had stopped. Captain Chapin at the first realization of the incident, had leaped up, and now stood scanning the water for the first glimpse of his sister when she would rise to the surface.

So great was the excitement on the naval launch that neither Dave nor Dan really noticed it when another man aboard the motor boat rose more slowly, showing his head for the first time above the gunwale.

As the motor boat put about on her course both Captain Chapin and this other man dived overboard.

"I wonder if they see Miss Chapin yet?" muttered Dave, as the naval launch raced to the scene.

It was speedily apparent that Miss Chapin had not yet been found, for both hatless swimmers swam about uncertainly, going down head first, from time to time, as though to explore the water near the surface.

Then the naval launch plunged into the scene. From it dived three ensigns and two sailors aboard who were not engaged with the handling of the craft.

With seven expert swimmers now in the water, Miss Lucy Chapin stood an excellent chance of being found.

Hardly had the Navy men dived when Captain Chapin's male companion swam with long overhand strokes away from the rest.

"I see her!" shouted this swimmer, and dived.

"He has her!" panted Dalzell. "Hooray!"

Instantly six swimmers turned and swam toward the rescuer, who now appeared on the surface supporting a woman's head on his shoulder.

"Good work! Fine!" cheered Dave.

Captain Chapin was the first to reach his sister's rescuer.

"Is Lucy dead?" cried Chapin anxiously, when he beheld his sister's white face.

"Stunned," replied the rescuer. "I think she must have been struck on the head by the boat as it passed her."

Silently the other swimmers turned in behind the young woman, her rescuer and brother.

"Better bring Miss Chapin to the 'Castoga's' boat, Captain," Dave called. "It's larger. We'll take her directly to the gunboat and have the surgeon attend her."

The boatswain's mate ran the naval launch up within easy distance, and Miss Chapin was lifted aboard.

On one of the cushions Miss Chapin was laid, while all gathered about her anxiously.

"Make the 'Castoga' with all speed," ordered Ensign Hale. "The young lady must have prompt attention."

On the way to the "Castoga" Captain Chapin did everything he could think of to revive his sister. The others stood about, ready to help.

Then it was that Dave happened, for the first time, to face the rescuer.

"Pembroke!" he called in astonishment.

"Howdy do?" asked the Englishman, with a smile holding out his hand.

Though Dave felt himself chilling with suspicion of the pleasant stranger, he could not withhold his hand.

"I was on my way out to visit your ship," smiled Pembroke, as he released Dave's hand after a warm grip. "Captain Chapin was good enough to say that he would present me on board."

"And glad indeed I am that I undertook to do so," exclaimed Chapin. "If it hadn't been for you, Pembroke, I am afraid my sister would have been lost."

Pembroke was now engaged in shaking hands with Dalzell, who felt obliged to present him to Ensign Hale.

"A splendid rescue, that," said Hale warmly.

The gunboat's launch was now speedily alongside the "Castoga," the motor boat, a small craft that carried passengers on the bay for hire, following at slower speed.

"We've a half-drowned young lady on board, who needs the surgeon's attention," called Hale, between his hands, just before the launch ran alongside.

Miss Chapin was immediately taken on board, and carried to the quarters of the executive officer, where she was laid in a bunk. Only her brother and the surgeon remained with her.

Dave felt obliged to introduce Pembroke to his brother officers. The Englishman proceeded to make their acquaintance with evident delight.

Five minutes later the executive officer recovered his presence of mind sufficiently to send ashore to Cavite for dry garments of a size suitable for Miss Chapin's use. In an hour or two that young lady, revived and attired in dry clothing, was brought on deck on her brother's arm. She was weak, but out of danger.

"We came out in order to make a call aboard," Captain Chapin explained to the officers under the quarter-deck awning, "but we had no idea we were going to make such a sensational visit."

"I fancy that women are always nuisances aboard naval craft," smiled Miss Chapin, whereupon the assembled officers promptly assured her that women were nothing of the sort.

In the meantime the three officers who had leaped over into the bay had had time to change their clothing. It became a merry party on deck.

Up to Mr. Warden stepped a messenger, saluting.

"The Lieutenant Commander's compliments, sir, and will the executive officer report to the Lieutenant Commander at once?"

"Immediately," replied Lieutenant Warden, returning the salute, taking his brief adieu by merely raising his uniform cap before he left the party.

Ten minutes later Lieutenant Warden stepped briskly on deck. He paused long enough to say something in an undertone to the officer of the deck, who smartly passed the word for a messenger.

"I am sorry to announce," said the executive officer, approaching the group of officers who surrounded Miss Chapin, "that our pleasant days in Manila are ended for the present."

"I should say so," cried Captain Chapin. "There goes your recall flag to the mast-head."

"Right!" replied Mr. Warden crisply. "Our sailing orders have just been wirelessed from shore. We sail at seven this evening, if our few men on shore leave can be recalled in that time. Mr. Hale, you are to take the launch and go ashore after the leave men."

"Very good, sir," replied that ensign, saluting, next raising his cap to Miss Chapin and hastening away.

"Leaving, are you?" asked Pembroke, in a tone of regret. "And what is your destination?"

"China," rejoined Lieutenant Warden tersely.

The Englishman's face changed expression.

"Not—" he stammered. "Not the—"

"For the Nung-kiang River," replied the executive officer.

Dave Darrin and Dan Dalzell were the only ones present who caught the strange, fleeting look that passed over the face of Pembroke.

"Why can this Englishman object to our going to the Nung-kiang River?" Ensign Darrin wondered. "What interest can he take in any mission of ours there?"

CHAPTER IV—THE LANDING PARTY AT NU-PING

"That ought to hold the pirates for a little while," declared Danny Grin, his good-natured face looking unusually grim.

"I think it will," replied Dave, halting before his cabin door. "Dan Dalzell, if my face is as dirty as yours I shouldn't care to walk up Main Street in my native town."

"Go in and look at *yourself*," scoffed Dalzell.

"It's fully as dirty," called Dave, from the interior of his cabin, surveying himself in the glass.

But it was as honorable dirt as any man may have on his face—the grime of powder-smoke as it blew back when the gunboat's five-inch guns had been swung open at the breech.

For the "Castoga," intercepted by wireless on the way to the Nung-kiang, had been sent to Hong Kong by an official order from Washington. The threatened troubles along the Nung-kiang had quieted down to such an extent that cautious officials in Washington dreaded lest Chinese sensibilities should be wounded by the sending of a gunboat up the river.

So, day after day, the "Castoga" had lain in the mountain-bordered harbor at Hong Kong.

Then came the word one day that the Chinese rebels in the district around the city of Nu-ping, on the Nung-kiang River, had again become troublesome, and that the American mission buildings at Nu-ping were threatened. The "Castoga" had been ordered to proceed at full speed, she being the nearest craft of a draft light enough to ascend the river.

During the last hours of darkness the gunboat had steamed up the river, all eyes on board turned toward the sinister red glow that lighted the sky above the Chinese city, capital of a province.

Just before daylight the gunboat dropped anchor with every man and officer at quarters.

From shore came the sound of rifle shots, a wild pandemonium of yells, as thousands of raging Chinese surged upon the mission buildings, to which fire had already been set, and from which the American missionaries and their families, aided by the white residents of Nu-ping, were making the only resistance that lay within their power.

The first note of cheer that came to the missionaries and their friends was the whistle of the gunboat, sounding clearly when still two miles distant. Then the lights of the fighting craft came into sight.

For a few minutes after coming to anchor, the commander of the "Castoga" was forced to wait for sufficient daylight to enable him to distinguish accurately between friend and foe.

At the side of the gunboat a launch and four cutters waited, to carry a landing party, if the sending ashore of men should prove to be necessary. Anxiously, using his night glasses every minute, the American commander paced the deck and listened.

Then, when there was barely enough light, word was telephoned to the division officers to begin action.

Boom! spoke the first gun from the gunboat. Other shots followed rapidly.

In the compound before the burning mission buildings was a mass of yellow fiends, crowding, yelling and shooting. From the windows of such portions of the burning buildings as were still tenable American rifle fire was poured into the mob.

That first shell, landing among the yellow fiends, killed more than twenty Mongols, wounded others, and drove the attackers out of the compound.

Boom! Bang! Other shells flew through the air, clearing away the rabble further back.

From the mission buildings, a quarter of a mile away, went up a wild cheer of hope.

But the attacking rabble, despite the first shell fire, came back, inviting further punishment.

Again the gunboat's five-inch guns roared out. There was now sufficient light to enable the American gunners to make out the locations of the mob.

At least thirty shells were fired ere the rebels beat a retreat beyond the confines of Nu-ping.

It was time to stop firing, for some of the American shells had set fire to Chinese dwellings and business buildings.

On a low hill, a quarter of a mile away from the burning mission buildings, flew the Chinese flag, flanked by the flag of the governor of the province.

Watching this yamen, or palace, the American officers saw a body of not more than a hundred soldiers issue suddenly from behind the walls. Straight to the mission hurried these tardy fighting men. Though late in acting, the Chinese governor was sending an invitation to the endangered missionaries and their friends to share the hospitality and protection of his yamen.

"He might have done that before," muttered Dan Dalzell.

"If he has so few Chinese soldiers," Dave explained, "he never could have driven back the thousands of rebels. Our friend, the governor, is cautious, surely, but plainly he is no fool."

Once the bombardment had stopped, the various officers, except one division officer, had been ordered to their quarters to clean up and put on fresh uniforms, for the work of the day was by no means finished.

So back to their quarters hurried the released division officers.

Dave Darrin quickly divested himself of his dungaree working clothes, then stripped entirely, going under a shower bath. From this he emerged and rubbed down, drew on fresh underclothing, a clean shirt, and hastily completed his toilet.

At that instant there came a summons at the door, with an order for Ensign Darrin to attire himself in khaki uniform. The same order was delivered to Dan.

"Landing party work," was the thought that leaped instantly into the minds of both.

Nor were they disappointed. Into the launch, with several other boats alongside, tumbled forty sailors and twelve marines, armed, and with rapid-fire guns and ammunition. In one of the other boats were additional cases of ammunition; in others were commissary supplies.

Dave received his orders from Executive Officer Warden.

"You will go ashore, Ensign Darrin, and at all hazards reach our fellow Americans. What you shall do on reaching them will depend upon circumstances and upon instructions signaled to you from this ship. Ensign Dalzell will accompany you as next in command. On board we shall keep vigilant watch, and you may rely upon such backing as our guns can give you in any emergency that may come up."

Dave saluted, with a hearty "Very good, sir," but asked no questions. None were necessary.

In another moment the landing party had been reinforced by a petty officer and three men who were to bring the boats back to the "Castoga."

Casting off, the launch headed shoreward, towing the boats astern.

Within three minutes, landing had been made at one of the smaller docks.

"I don't see any reception committee here to welcome us," muttered Ensign Dalzell.

"Probably all of the natives, who are curious by nature, are watching the burning of the buildings that our shells set on fire," returned Ensign Darrin. "But I'm glad there's no reception party here, for undoubtedly it would be an armed committee."

As soon as landing had been effected, however, a petty officer, who was sent forward with three men, succeeded in routing out a number of sturdy, sullen coolies, who had been hiding in a near-by warehouse. These yellow men the petty officer marched back briskly, the coolies being forced to pick up and carry the ammunition and food supplies.

"See to it that these Chinese don't try to run away with the stuff," Dave ordered tersely. "Keep them under close guard."

"Aye, aye, sir."

At the word from Darrin, Dalzell ordered the sailors to fall in and lead the way in double file, the marines marching at the rear of the little baggage train.

"Straight to the yamen!" commanded Darrin, as he gave Dan the forward order, then fell back to keep an eye over the conduct of the porters.

For the first block of the march through the narrow, foul-smelling streets, the natives contented themselves with glancing sullenly out at the handful of daring invaders. But a turn in the street brought the American naval men in sight of an angry-looking crowd of nearly a thousand Chinese—all men.

"Are they going to block our way?" whispered Dan, marching quietly on when Dave hastened to his side.

"They are not," Darrin answered bluntly, "though they may try to. No one is going to block us to-day until we have used all our ammunition."

"That has the good old Yankee sound," grinned Dalzell.

Seeing that the sullen crowd was massing, Ensign Darrin went forward, hastening in advance of his little column.

"Is there any one here who speaks English?" Dave called pleasantly, above the dead hush of that stolid Chinese crowd.

There was no answer.

"All right then," smiled Ensign Darrin, "I shall have to talk to you by sign language. Make way, please!"

Drawing his sword, he signed to the Chinese to make way for his command to pass. Still no response.

Ensign Dan, marching his men on, came up to Dave's side.

"Column halt!" Ensign Darrin called promptly. "Order arms. Draw bayonets. Fix bayonets!"

With a rattling of steel, accompanied by many grins, sailors and marines alike obeyed.

"Once more, I call upon you to make way!" called Dave, striding forward and endeavoring to wave the crowd aside by gestures with his sword. Still nobody moved.

"Ensign Dalzell," rapped out the sharp order, "form two platoons extending across the street in close order. Give promptly the order to charge."

As he gave this command Darrin stepped back, placing himself at the extreme right of the first short platoon.

"Charge bayonets!" ordered Dan.

Dave led the men forward, Dalzell remaining behind with the remainder of the little command.

Finding the points of the bayonets at their breasts, the Chinese gave utterance to cries of fright. There was a backward surge.

"Halt!" cried Dave, just in time to prevent some of the Chinese from feeling cold American steel. "Steady! Forward march! Hep, hep, hep!"

Emphasizing the speed of the step with his "hep, hep," Dave now continued his squad at a brisk walk, giving the yellow natives time to make their retreat without trampling one another.

At the next corner the Chinese surged off at right angles in two directions.

"I guess we'll find the rest of the way clear enough," smiled Ensign Dave, again forming his men in double file and falling back to Dan's side. "The Mongols had me scared. I was afraid I'd have to order the men to load and fire."

"Would you have done that?" asked Dalzell.

"Why not?" asked Dave, with a shrug of his shoulders. "There are American women up at the yamen, and they are still in peril. My orders are to reach the yamen, and I propose to do it if it be possible. If any yellow men try to block our way they will do so at their own risk. I'll charge or fire into any crowd or force that blocks our way."

"Good!" chuckled Ensign Dan. "I like the sound of that talk!"

Down by the river front, save for the warehouses, the buildings were of the meanest—flimsy affairs of bamboo, with cheaply lacquered facings, windows of oiled paper and floors of earth. Now, however, the little naval column began to pass through a better part of the city. Here the houses were of wood, substantially built, and of pagoda or tent patterns. Not a few of these dwellings were surrounded by compounds, or yards, enclosed by high stone walls.

And then, at last, in the heart of the city, the column came out upon the low hillside on which was the great square surrounding the governor's yamen.

None in front opposed Darrin's command, but a crowd that must have numbered two thousand followed close at the heels of the detachment.

"Going to halt in the center of the square?" Dan inquired in a low tone.

"No," rejoined Ensign Dave. "I shall march up to the main gate in the compound wall."

"And then—?" inquired Dalzell.

"I shall demand to be admitted to the American refugees."

"And if you are refused?" pressed Dan.

"That will be the governor's worry," replied Dave quietly.

CHAPTER V—SIN FOO HAS HIS DOUBTS

It was a gray stone wall, some twelve feet high, that surrounded the compound of the yamen. Sentries in the uniform of Chinese soldiery were pacing the top of this formidable rampart.

Over the walls could be seen the strange, gracefully arched red and yellow roofs of the several large and the few small buildings of the yamen.

Under the gray walls, on the outside, crouched a few mangy-looking beggars. Men and women of this type always loiter outside of every yamen, trusting to the occasional generosity of the high official who resides within, for in China every mandarin, governor and other high official must always be a good deal of an alms-giver.

Not even the sight of the heavily armed little American column stirred these beggars beyond the most ordinary exhibition of curiosity.

"Put the column to the right oblique, and go over to that gate," directed Dave, pointing with his drawn sword.

A moment later the command, "Halt!" rang out. From the ramparts above three Chinese soldiers gazed down stolidly.

Striding forward to the gong that hung before the gate, Ensign Darrin struck it loudly three times.

A minute passed without answer. Dave sounded thrice again. Another minute passed.

"Confound those fellows inside," muttered Dave to his chum. "I've heard, before this, that the Chinese official tries to show his contempt for western barbarians by making them await his pleasure."

Glancing down his line, Darrin noted a sailor who was well known for his physical powers.

"Henshaw!" summoned Dave crisply.

Leaving the ranks, Seaman Henshaw stepped briskly forward, saluting respectfully.

"Henshaw, do you think you could play a loud tune on this gong?"

"Aye, aye, sir."

"How long do you think you could keep that tune going?"

"An hour, anyway, sir."

"Can you play that gong like a bass-drum?"

"Like a whole drum-corps, sir," answered Seaman Henshaw, with just the suspicion of a grin.

"Then fall to, Henshaw."

Picking up the fancifully carved stick, Seaman Henshaw faced the three-foot gong.

Bang! crash! zim! zoum! smash! It was a lusty tattoo that Seaman Henshaw beat upon that resounding metal. *The noise could have been heard a mile away.* Dave afterwards learned that every sound was distinctly heard on board the gunboat.

26

It Could Have Been Heard a Mile Away.

Bim! bam! whang! After a full minute of it Seaman Henshaw looked as if he were still enjoying his task. Several of the men in the waiting column had grounded their rifle butts that they might hold at least one hand to an ear to shut out the din.

On the wall overhead the Chinese sentries moved uneasily away from close quarters.

Crash! zam! bing! That gong rang forth as, it is safe to say, it had not done before in centuries, for Henshaw was a young giant and proud of his muscle and endurance.

Zim! zim! zam! The racket was more than ears could endure for a long stretch.

At about the end of the third minute the double gates were thrown suddenly open. In the open gateway stood at least a score of armed soldiers, at their head a young Chinaman, tall, well-dressed and of rather commanding appearance.

Instantly Ensign Darrin pressed Henshaw's unemployed arm. With a final crash the pounding of the gong died out.

"His excellency, the governor, demands to know why this din is being made at this gate," declared the tall young Chinaman, in a haughty voice, but in excellent English.

"It is my way of announcing my call," Dave replied.

"Who are you?"

"Ensign Darrin, United States Navy, very much at your service, sir," Dave replied. "And now, sir, I have the honor to request that you, also, announce your name and position here."

"Since I serve his excellency, the governor, that is enough for you to know," replied the Chinaman. "However, I will state that my name is Sin Foo. I am under secretary to his excellency, and, as such, I have come to bring word to you that it is his excellency's pleasure that you depart from this neighborhood and return to your vessel."

"I am very sorry, Mr. Sin Foo," Dave responded, "but it is impossible for me to make my call on a proxy. I must see his excellency in person."

"I am very sorry," replied the secretary, speaking in a tone of cold contempt, "but his excellency cannot see you so early in the day. Later—"

"Attention," called Ensign Dave, in a low voice. "Column, forward march!"

Instantly the naval line moved forward. Shocked and indignant, the secretary spoke in Chinese to some of the soldiers. The big gate began to move as though it would shut.

"At the double quick! Charge!" shouted Dave Darrin, leaping forward, brandishing his sword.

In a twinkling the first dozen seamen, headed by two officers, had rushed into the compound.

At one side stood two Chinese soldiers, working a cumbersome wheel, attached to a windlass and rope that moved the double gate. Henshaw leaped at this pair, knocking both down.

"I must warn you, Ensign Darrin," shouted Sin Foo, his face purple with rage, "that this conduct of yours is contrary to the usages of respect that must be observed between the representatives of two great countries. Your conduct, sir, is an outrage!"

"And the governor's conduct also is an outrage," Darrin retorted sternly, "in allowing mobs to burn the mission buildings and all but take the lives of the American missionaries and their families."

"All the mission Americans are safe at this yamen," retorted Sin Foo. "There is no need to fear for your fellow Americans. They are safe and under the immediate protection of his excellency, the governor."

"That is what I have come to see about," Dave declared. "Mr. Sin Foo, I have no wish to be lacking in courtesy, and I shall display as much as I can, under the circumstances. But my men are now inside the compound, and here they will remain until my orders are changed by my commanding officer."

Though the Chinese soldiers had withdrawn to varying distances before the harmless bayonet rush, Sin Foo remained and faced Ensign Darrin with every sign of indignant disapproval in his almond-shaped eyes.

The impressed Chinese porters had been driven into the compound, where they dropped their burdens. Dan quietly paid them off with silver coins. The instant they found themselves permitted to leave, these sullen coolies fairly flew out through the still open gate.

"Sir," began Sin Foo again, speaking with great haughtiness, "if these supplies are intended for the American missionaries, I will undertake to receive them on behalf of your countrymen, but I must once more, and for the last time, insist that you withdraw your men from this compound. If you do not instantly withdraw, it will provoke grave trouble between your country and mine."

"Mr. Sin Foo," Dave replied, speaking pleasantly, and smiling, "I wish to treat you, and all other Chinese officials with every mark of courtesy. I must make it plain, however, that I shall not leave this yamen until I have been so ordered by my commanding officer. Moreover, I am under strict orders to see the American mission party at once, and I must very respectfully insist upon no more delay. I demand, sir, to see Bishop Whitlock first of all."

"Ensign Darrin, your language is insolent!" cried Sin Foo angrily.

"My talk will quickly change to acts, if my requests are not at once granted," replied Dave, firmly.

"'Acts'? What do you mean by that word?" demanded Sin Foo.

"I mean that if Bishop Whitlock and his friends are not at once produced, I shall be under the necessity of searching the yamen for them," Ensign Darrin rejoined.

"Search the yamen?" gasped Sin Foo incredulously. "Would you dare profane the sovereignty of China?"

"I'll do it in just five minutes, if my request is not heeded," retorted Ensign Dave drawing out his watch.

By this time at least one hundred and fifty armed Chinese soldiers had appeared, on the ramparts, in the compound, in the doorways and windows of the buildings. Darrin's force was much inferior numerically. Sudden treachery on the part of the Chinese might cut the American naval force in two, but Danny Grin was keeping alert watch on all Chinese in sight.

"You are making a grave mis—" began Sin Foo loftily.

"And you have already lost forty-five seconds of that five minutes," Ensign Dave suggested, still standing, watch in hand. "If you use up the time in conversation, Mr. Sin Foo, I shall not grant a grace of even five seconds."

"Your insolence, sir, overwhelms me," replied the under secretary. "Shudderingly, I shall take it into the presence of his excellency."

"And impress upon his excellency, if you please, that I am not going to lose time," answered Dave, again glancing at his watch.

Turning on his heel, Sin Foo disappeared through a near-by door of one of the buildings.

Several minutes slipped by. Dave glanced frequently at the hands of his watch.

"The time is nearly up, Dan," he announced, at last. "You remain in command of the marines and guard our ammunition and other stores. At the second of five minutes I shall form the sailormen and march through this yamen until I find the missionary party."

Danny Grin nodded gravely.

"Seamen fall in!" called Ensign Darrin, replacing his watch in his pocket. "Forward, guard left, mar—"

"Stop!" cried a ringing voice. Out of the doorway through which he had vanished appeared Sin Foo, running and waving his arms.

"The governor's answer?" Dave curtly demanded, turning upon his heel.

"I will take you to the missionary party," conceded Sin Foo.

"Very well; step with me, then, and lead the way."

"But you must not take an armed party with you," protested Sin Foo, looking very much aghast.

"My men go with me," Dave replied firmly. "Sir, we cannot have any more nonsense. I am convinced that my countrymen must be prisoners, else they would have come out to greet me before this. Lead the way and I will march my men behind you."

Looking as though he would very much like to say a good deal, Sin Foo led the way around the buildings to the left, thence to the farthest building of all at the rear of the compound. Scattered around the outside of this building were nearly a score of Chinese soldiers carrying their rifles at shoulder arms.

"You have kept the Americans as prisoners, just as I suspected," charged Ensign Darrin, turning accusingly upon the under secretary.

"And you forget, Ensign Darrin," retorted Sin Foo, "that his excellency the governor commands here."

"We'll let it go at that," answered the young ensign, "provided your governor doesn't attempt to put any crimps in the safety or liberty of my countrymen. Right now, be good enough to order your soldiers away so that there may be no clash between them and my men."

Through the windows of the one-story building Dave Darrin could see several faces of men and women looking eagerly out.

Sullenly, Sin Foo spoke to the Chinese soldiers, who, saluting, withdrew to a distance, though they did not leave the scene. Then a door was flung open, and American citizens began to pour out.

Darting through the foremost of the throng was one handsome young American woman, who, holding her arms outstretched, while eager tears of gladness glistened in her eyes, cried:

"Dave!"

It was Belle Darrin, once Belle Meade, Dave's schoolgirl sweetheart then, and now his wife.

"You, Belle?" he exclaimed, almost incredulously, as he embraced her. "I thought you were in Manila, awaiting word when and where to join me."

30

"I couldn't wait any longer to join you, so I came up in the last steamer from Manila, and transferred to a river boat at the foot of the river. Aren't you glad to see me?"

"Glad, indeed!" Dave embraced her again. But he was on duty, and most urgent duty at that. Even further conversation with his beloved wife must wait until he had rightful leisure.

Then his eye fell upon another in the little throng.

"You here, Mr. Pembroke?" Ensign Darrin inquired.

"Yes," confessed the Englishman. "I'm a bit of a rover, you know. Never know where I shall be next."

"And Mr. Pembroke has been extremely kind in helping me on the journey," Belle added brightly. "Mr. Pembroke told me that he had met you in Manila."

Though Dave bowed courteously he couldn't help feeling dislike of this smooth-talking Pembroke. The latter was an Englishman; then, unless he was serving his country in this part of the world, why wasn't the fellow at home, doing his bit of military service for Britain? He was young enough, and able-bodied, and England was calling all her younger men to the colors. To Darrin's mind it was a sheer confession of disgrace for Pembroke to admit that he was merely touring the world at a time when England was demanding service on the battle field from every young Briton who was not otherwise engaged in serving his country.

"When you have time, Mr. Darrin, I'll claim just a word of greeting," said a soft voice, and a gloved hand was held out to Dave.

"So you came through also, Miss Chapin?" Dave inquired, as he took Lucy Chapin's hand.

"I'm glad to see you, but sorry you're here," rejoined Dave.

"Why sorry to see me here?" inquired Miss Chapin. "Aren't we now under the protection of the American Navy?"

"Every sailorman on the 'Castoga' will die willingly in defense of this party," Darrin told her, "but the trouble may easily assume such proportions that our little force will prove wholly inadequate."

Then, glancing swiftly over the missionary party, the young naval officer added:

"Will some one kindly introduce me to Bishop Whitlock?"

As Dave had expected, it was one of the three white-haired men of the party who now pressed forward. Mrs. Darrin introduced her husband to the bishop.

"You reached us not a bit too early," the bishop assured Dave.

"You were practically prisoners in the yamen, sir?" Dave asked.

"Almost, I fear, though we refused to give up our arms. Even now seven of our men are inside keeping guard over our weapons."

"How many rifles do you have?" Dave asked.

"Thirty-two," answered the bishop promptly. "The American residents of the city flocked to our defense."

"From what I saw from the ship's deck," rejoined Darrin, "all I can say is that you presented a magnificent front with only thirty-two rifles. As I have but fifty-two naval rifles with me, that makes up a total force of only eighty-four rifles."

"Can't we get through to the water-front?" inquired Belle. "For you are going to take us to the 'Castoga,' are you not?"

"If we can safely get there," Dave replied. "And now I must drop everything else until I have communicated with the gunboat. Bishop, did you lose any of your party?"

"None of the white members," replied the missionary. "Our sixteen Chinese converts at the mission insisted on taking care of themselves. Whether any of them has been killed, I do not know."

"I must get a signalman up on the walls," Dave continued. "Bishop, will you kindly see, sir, that your party follows my men? I am going to the other side of the compound."

As soon as Belle Darrin caught sight of her old school friend, Danny Grin, she hurried forward to greet him.

Out of the main building of the yamen came Sin Foo, with sullen, offended face and stately tread.

"Sir," called Dave, "I must put a signalman up on the ramparts."

"Since you take everything into your own hands," replied the secretary coldly, "you do not need his excellency's permission. Yet I am charged to say that all you do here is against the protest of his excellency, and complaint will be made to your government."

"I am sorry, sir, to seem to show discourtesy," Ensign Dave replied, "but all that I do here is under general instructions from the highest representative of my government in these waters."

With that Dave called a signalman to him, gave him a message, and directed six other sailors to climb, with the signalman, the inside steps that led to the rampart.

No sooner had the signalman, in the lead, gained the rampart, than a five-inch gun on the "Castoga" boomed out.

"Ensign Darrin, sir," bawled down the signalman lustily, "I think you will be glad to be up here, to see what is going on."

Dropping Belle's hand, which he had just taken, Ensign Dave darted up the steps, uttering, on reaching the top of the stone wall, an exclamation of dismay.

"Ensign Dalzell!" he shouted, beckoning the summons to his brother officer.

CHAPTER VI—HECKLING HIS EXCELLENCY

"Jupiter!" gasped Dan, as he reached Dave's side.

Boom! bang! Two shots were fired almost together from the "Castoga's" forward guns.

"The rebels are returning from the suburbs," Dave exclaimed, "and even the near-by houses are emptying themselves of hundreds of other armed men."

"There must be a million of them, in all," said Danny Grin briefly, "but I reckon we can thrash 'em all."

"We'll have to, or go under," was Dave's brief retort. "There cannot be a doubt that the armed multitude intends to attack the yamen."

In the meantime Signalman Ross was sending the message that Dave had given him. Now a signalman on the gunboat wig-wagged back:

"Do not attempt to leave yamen with your party until you receive orders so to do."

"I'm glad of that command," Dave muttered to his subordinate. "I wouldn't care to risk any of our American women by trying to take them through such a rabble as I see advancing."

Again some of the "Castoga's" guns spoke. The shell fire was doing some execution in the ranks of the oncoming rebels, though not enough to halt their march.

"I am going down into the compound to send up men and rapid-fire guns," Dave announced to his chum. "Post the men, and station one rapid-fire gun on each of the four sides of the compound."

"What are you going to do with the Chinese soldiers?" Dan asked.

Dave frowned.

"I don't know," he said. "This is the governor's yamen, and these are his troops. I don't believe we can trust them, but, on the other hand, have we any right to drive the soldiers out? And would they go peaceably, or would they open fire and put the women in danger?"

"Ask the Captain, by signal," Dan advised.

"Ask him yourself, signing my name, Dan. Whatever we do, the rapid-fire guns can't be placed on these walls a moment too soon."

Hustling below, Dave ordered up the sailors and all but four of the marines. Each man, as he went, carried up a case of one thousand cartridges, either for the rapid-fire guns or for the infantry rifles.

"You men in charge of the stores," Dave ordered, "keep the Chinese away from our property. Don't let any of the yellow men touch the stores. Shoot before you permit that, and shoot promptly and to kill!"

Then Darrin turned his attention to the missionary party. Of the thirty-two men who carried rifles, he sent twenty to the ramparts, while he directed the other twelve to stand guard over the women.

Having made these dispositions of his command, Ensign Darrin again raced up to the top of the wall.

"There's the answer just coming from the gunboat," Dan informed him. So Dave, shading his eyes with one hand, picked up this message from the "Castoga":

"Ensign Darrin: You will need to exercise great caution as to what you do in the yamen, as only the presence of imperilled missionary party justifies presence of your command there at all. Better consult with the governor."

"That's just what I'll do," Dave uttered grimly. "That governor chap has been keeping himself mighty well out of sight. Now it's time for me to see him, and he must show up and take some little hand in affairs that are going on in his city and province."

"Shall I allow more Chinese soldiers up here on the wall?" asked Ensign Dalzell. "Here they come."

That was, indeed, only too true. Very quietly, under their own officers, some hundred and sixty of the governor's troops had formed in four detachments, going to the walls at the four sides of the compound and starting up the steps.

"I don't know whether we can stop them, and I don't know that they won't be willing to fight with us and for us," returned Darrin, perplexedly. "I'll follow the commander's orders and see the governor at once."

Running down, and darting across the compound, Dave halted before the principal door of the main building, the door Sin Foo had used.

Knocking lustily with the hilt of his sword, Dave did not wait more than thirty seconds. Then reports from two more of the gunboat's guns decided him. He seized the latch, trying to force the door, but only to find that barrier locked.

"Open!" ordered Dave, in his loudest quarterdeck voice. "Open!"

He waited another thirty seconds, but no one inside obeyed.

"Open," he shouted, "or I shall order my men to batter the door down!"

Inside, instantly, he heard the murmur of voices.

"Well," demanded the irate young officer, "will you open, or do you wish the door battered down?"

Preceded by a rattling of bolt chains, the great door was thrown open. Into the doorway breach stepped Sin Foo, calmly disdainful. Behind him stood fully a score of Chinese soldiers, each with rifle leveled ready to shoot.

"Why this unseemly disturbance before the official residence of the governor?" demanded Sin Foo.

"I must see the governor immediately," Dave replied.

"It will be impossible to see his excellency, except upon appointment," replied the secretary. "His excellency's presence is sacred, and is not to be invaded at will by a hasty caller with sword in hand. If you will wait here, I will ascertain if his excellency will be pleased to see you in an hour."

"If he keeps me waiting two minutes," Ensign Dave retorted, "I shall search this building for him."

"At your first step inside," Sin Foo proclaimed, "these soldiers will fire upon you. That will be the signal for all our troops to fire on your men, who are no better than unlawful invaders."

"Ensign Dalzell!" shouted Dave, over his shoulder.

"Aye, aye, sir."

"Rush six men here, with the machine gun from the river side of the wall!"

"Very good, sir!" came in Dan's delighted voice.

No sooner did he comprehend than Sin Foo uttered something in Chinese. Through the squad of soldiers darted half a dozen yellow servants who instantly sought to close the door.

"Back with you!" ordered Darrin, whipping out his revolver and menacing the frightened servants.

"If the word to start killing is given it will really come from you, Mr. Sin Foo," Dave warned the secretary sternly, "and you will be one of the first men to drop dead."

Dave's foot was now posted where it would obstruct the closing of the door, even if attempted.

"Here we are, sir," panted a sailor, darting up with a machine gun and its crew.

"Train your gun to cover this corridor," Dave ordered, tersely.

The gun captain posted the machine gun so that its nose pointed at the squad of Chinese.

"Withdraw those soldiers, Mr. Sin Foo!" briefly commanded Ensign Darrin.

"What?" gasped the thunderstruck under secretary. "You presume to give orders in the governor's very residence?"

"I don't intend to argue," Dave retorted, as another of the "Castoga's" guns spoke from the river. "If you don't run your soldiers out of this corridor, then the janitor will have them to sweep out, for I'm going to order the machine gun into action mighty soon!"

Sin Foo looked puzzled, but soon he spoke to the soldiers, who, scowling, wheeled and marched back down the stone-flagged corridor, vanishing around an angle of the wall.

"The governor will not see you, sir," Sin Foo insisted.

"You're wrong there, too," Dave crisped out. "It was my wish to be courteous. But now I have the honor to tell you that the governor will come to the doorway to speak with me, and he'll come very promptly, or else I shall march a force of men into the house and find him. It will be much pleasanter for his excellency if he promptly decides to come here. Mr. Sin Foo, you have my permission to go and tell him just what I have said."

For perhaps thirty seconds the under secretary stood gazing at the ensign. On his face was a look of absolute horror. During the pause Dave eyed him sternly.

"I mean business, Mr. Sin Foo!"

"Ensign Darrin, though it be at the cost of my head, which I can ill afford to spare," murmured Sin Foo brokenly, "I shall undertake to bear to his excellency's shocked ears your most outrageous message."

Turning to his sailors, who were grinning discreetly, Dave Darrin observed softly:

"I think that will put motion into the governor's feet, if anything will."

Looking frequently at his watch, Ensign Dave waited a full two minutes.

"Come on, men," he ordered, "we'll start through the premises. This isn't the time even to wait for governors."

Some ten yards down the corridor Darrin had led his handful of men when Sin Foo's shocked voice rang out:

"Halt! Stop! Outraged as his excellency feels, he is coming to listen for himself to your impertinence."

"Halt!" ordered Dave, in a low tone. Again the machine gun was set up. But this time no delay was attempted. The same score of soldiers marched around the angle, halted and formed on either side of the corridor. Next came Ah Sin Foo, with tablet, ink and writing brush, while a servant carried a small table.

Behind them came five more officials, then one whom, from his elaborate Chinese costume, Darrin took to be the governor. After that personage came several other men.

Suddenly Dave Darrin started perceptibly. Among the governor's followers, richly dressed, was none other than Mr. "Burnt-face," lately of Manila!

"Now, what the mischief can 'Burnt-face' be doing here?" Darrin gasped inwardly. "And, by the same token, what was he really doing in Manila?"

"Step out and get two or three of the missionaries who understand Chinese," Dave ordered in a low voice to the sailor nearest him.

Striking his hands together for silence, the Chinese governor sank down upon a richly carved chair which a yamen servant placed for him. Then he addressed Sin Foo in Chinese.

"His excellency demands to know the meaning of this extraordinary conduct," translated the under secretary.

"Ask his excellency if he is aware that the city is now alive with rioters?" requested Dave.

There was some conversation in Chinese, after which Sin Foo replied:

"His excellency says that his troops are upon the walls of the yamen ramparts."

"Does his excellency believe that his troops are going to be able to defeat the thousands of rioters who are marching here rapidly?" Dave asked.

After more conversation in Chinese Sin Foo explained:

"His excellency says he will guarantee the safety of all within the yamen precincts."

"Even if the rebels attack resolutely?" Dave insisted.

"In spite of any attack," Sin Foo assured him.

The missionaries who had been sent for were entering, but ahead of them darted a sailor who saluted the young officer and cried:

"Ensign Dalzell reports, sir, that the ramparts are being fired upon from the streets beyond. Ensign Dalzell believes, sir, that a general attack upon the yamen is about to begin."

"Tell Ensign Dalzell," Dave answered, "that he is to open fire as soon and as heavily as he deems best."

Then, to the astounded under secretary Darrin added:

"I must beg his excellency to go with me to the ramparts."

"He cannot—will not," protested Sin Foo.

"He *must!*" declared Dave Darrin firmly.

CHAPTER VII—BELLE HAS SOME "TIPS"

Whatever Sin Foo said, it was spoken in an undertone.

Near his excellency there was movement among the members of his retinue. In another instant the governor had vanished around the angle in the wall.

"Grab that 'Burnt-face' chap!" whispered Dave, to two of his sailors. "Hurry him along to the ramparts, but don't be rough with him unless you have to be."

Then up to Sin Foo, in the same twinkling, stepped Ensign Darrin.

"Sir, I am sorry, but I haven't time to waste on formal speech. Since your governor has run away, you must go with me to the ramparts."

"But I—I am not a fighting man," protested Sin Foo, turning to a greenish hue, which in a Mongol, is equivalent to turning pale.

"I believe you," assented Darrin. "And you won't be very much of any sort of man, unless you make up your mind to do instantly what I wish of you. Come!"

Nodding to a sailor to escort the under secretary, Dave and two of his men brought up the rear and rushed out into the open.

Left alone without command, the governor's score of soldiers, lined up against the walls, after a bewildered pause shuffled off in the wake of their departed chief.

Cr-r-rack! On the rampart at the west of the compound a squad of sailors had opened fire on a party of Chinese who were firing from the shelter of the nearest houses. Dan ran over to them, and stood behind his marksmen before Darrin succeeded in reaching the top of the steps nearest to the firing party.

At the outer edge of the rampart was a low wall of stone some two feet in thickness. On the flat floor behind this the sailors had thrown themselves, aiming their rifles over the parapet. Behind them Danny Grin, sword in hand, took position, pointing out some of the places of concealment of yellow snipers.

"They've opened fire, sir," reported Dalzell, saluting as his chum came up.

"So I see," nodded Ensign Dave. "Men, don't shoot too hastily. Try to plant every bullet where it will be most effective."

"Aye, aye, sir!" came the hearty chorus. Cr-r-r-rack!

Half a dozen of the missionaries who had joined the sailors on this part of the rampart, were proving their manhood by doing careful, deliberate work with their rifles. While under other circumstances these men of the cloth would have preferred not to take a hand in such an affair as this, the danger that threatened a score of American women completely changed their viewpoint.

"These mission men and the other American residents are going to make as good fighting material as you can get out of untrained men," Dave remarked to Dan, in a low voice.

Suddenly the "Castoga" took a lively hand in the affair again, her guns belching forth shells.

"Why, they're landing shells in the ruins of the mission settlement," declared Danny Grin. "What on earth can that be for?"

"I can't guess," answered Dave training his glass on the mission ruins. "Look! there are Chinamen, with shovels, running away. Have they been trying to intrench there?"

"Digging," answered a quiet voice behind the young officers, and Dave, turning, beheld the white hair and venerable face of Bishop Whitlock. "They are seeking the treasure, or were, until the gunboat shelled them out of our old compound."

"What treasure, sir?" Dave asked.

"Some Chinaman, either a simpleton or a mischief-maker, started the story that we missionaries had robbed a famous and very ancient temple at Sian-lio-Kung of a hidden treasure there, amounting to several million dollars' worth of gold and jewels, and that we had hidden the treasure by burying it in our own compound."

"There was no truth in that, sir?" asked Ensign Darrin incredulously.

"Not a bit, of course," replied the Bishop, smiling wearily. "Our entire treasure, in wealth, consisted of about seven hundred dollars in gold, belonging to our mission treasury. That gold is now hidden on the persons of men in my party."

37

Right over the top of his head Ensign Darrin felt something click. Then, conscious that something had happened, he turned, to see his cap, shot from his head, sailing down into the compound. A marine below picked it up and ran up the steps to hand it to his commander.

Belle Darrin saw the hat shot away, for in the compound below, she had stood watching her husband closely. She gave a slight start, but showed no other sign of fear.

A moment later a number of bullets swept over the rampart top. Dave, Dan and the Bishop were the only ones standing there. As for Sin Foo and "Burnt-face," they were grovelling on the rampart floor.

"Sir, I beg you to go below," Ensign Darrin urged the Bishop. "Or else lie flat. You are in too great danger here. I believe that the fire will soon be ten times more brisk, and considerably more deadly."

"I am not afraid," replied Bishop Whitlock calmly. "If my eyes were younger and keener I would handle a rifle, but I fear that I would waste too many cartridges."

"Won't you go below, sir, that we may all feel easier?" Dave begged.

"If I am making you uneasy, then I shall go down at once," answered the missionary simply. "My friend, may you be fortunate and successful here to-day!"

He held out a hand which Ensign Darrin grasped. Then the old man started below.

"The Chinese are starting firing from the river side," Dave announced, as a heavy volley of shots rang out from a new point. "Dan, you had better go over and direct our reply to the fire from the river side. Don't let any of the yellow rascals get close to the compound."

Dave turned just in time to see Sin Foo crawling down the steps, while "Burnt-face" looked on with evident interest.

"Mr. Sin Foo," Dave rasped out sharply, "come back! If you make another attempt to leave this rampart you will be fired upon without challenge. Any of my men who see you make the attempt will shoot you without further orders."

His fright showing to a ghastly degree, Sin Foo slowly crawled back. He was not in the slightest danger so long as he did not raise his head above the parapet, but the under secretary plainly had no military blood in his veins.

As for the Chinese soldiers on the ramparts, none of them displayed curiosity, nor had they shown any intention of attacking the Americans. It looked as though these yellow fighting men of the governor's did not regard it as being in any way their fight. Several of them were smoking pipes that gave off villainous odors.

Leaving a petty officer in charge, with general instructions, Dave went over to Dan's side of the compound.

"Your husband is showing magnificent courage," remarked Bishop Whitlock to Mrs. Darrin.

"My husband has been trained in the greatest fighting school in the world," Belle answered, "and I am certain that he is conducting himself according to the best traditions of his training and service."

A sailor came nimbly down with a message from Dave to the marines to open some of the food supplies and to start the preparation of a meal. In case the ladies were ready to eat, the marines were instructed to serve them first.

"How long since you Navy men have eaten?" Belle asked the sailor.

"Supper-time, last night, ma'am," replied the sailor, grinning.

"Then we women cannot think of eating until you men are taken care of," Belle replied, with emphasis.

"Not one of our men would eat until the ladies have eaten, ma'am," replied the sailor respectfully. "Ask that sea-going soldier there."

"When there are ladies with our parties, ma'am, they always have to be looked after first, ma'am," said the marine, straightening up.

"There are enough women here to serve every one at the same time," replied Belle Darrin. "Ladies, come here and help, if you please."

There were only crude implements with which to prepare food, but a supply of wood was brought and preparations for a meal went rapidly forward.

With only sixty-eight riflemen to guard all four sides of the yamen, and twenty of these civilians, Dave's task of defense was not an easy one.

At times spurts of rifle fire swept the ramparts, though so far none of the rebels had attempted to rush the yamen.

"Remember, men," Dave urged, as he passed along behind the firing parties, "your great task is to keep the heathen from rushing us. Make every cartridge count, but don't expose yourselves unnecessarily so long as the enemy are content to keep close to cover. Unless they succeed in making numerous hits, I don't believe they will try to rush us in daylight."

"But to-night, sir?" spoke up one of the petty officers.

"I hope that we shall have a chance to get out of here before nightfall," Ensign Darrin answered.

"It will be a miracle, if we do get out of here safely before nightfall," muttered the same petty officer, as Dave passed on to another part of the defenses.

After a while the firing died down. Dave ordered strict watch kept, but directed that there be no unnecessary firing until the Chinese beyond opened up heavily again.

Then, in the lull, he descended to the compound, to see to the care of the women, and afterwards of the men.

Standing aside, talking with a group of women, was Pembroke. That young man had made no effort to secure a rifle; he had not even offered his services toward the defense.

At the first opportunity Darrin walked aside with his wife.

"Mr. Pembroke came up from Manila with you?" he asked.

"On the same ship, yes," replied Belle.

"And came up on the same river boat with you?"

"Yes."

"Did Pembroke go to the mission to live?"

"He was there a part of the time," replied Belle. "He also lived elsewhere in Nu-ping some of the time. One day, I remember, I saw him on the street with a Chinaman who had a peculiar purple mark on his face under the right eye."

"Did you know that that same Chinaman, with the purple mark, is here at the yamen now?" Dave asked.

"Why, yes; after we were shut up in the building at the back of the compound, this morning, Mr. Pembroke went outside for a while, and afterwards I saw him talking with that same Chinaman with the purple mark on his face. Why are you asking all these questions, Dave?"

"Because I am puzzled about Pembroke," Dave replied. "At Manila I had an intimation that Pembroke is far from being a gentleman. At Manila, too, 'Burnt-face' was in evidence; if he were in Manila now he would be arrested, charged with the murder of another Chinaman. I have been doing some hard thinking, Belle. Suppose Pembroke knew that trouble with rebels was about to break out here at Nu-ping? He did know that the 'Castoga' was the gunboat in eastern waters best fitted for ascending the Nung-kiang River and that she was going there. Pembroke tried hard to make my acquaintance and to force himself upon me. Did he figure on being able to use me to advantage when the 'Castoga' was ordered to duty at this port, where he may have known that the rebellion was about to be sprung? To go further, were and are Pembroke and 'Burnt-face' pals and comrades, working together for some sinister purpose?"

Belle looked puzzled as she replied slowly:

"Bishop Whitlock attributes the present trouble to the spreading of a foolish story that in the mission grounds were buried millions of dollars' worth of treasure, looted from an ancient Chinese temple. What connection could Pembroke and his Chinese friend, away down in Manila, possibly have with such a stupid fable as that?"

"They may have believed the story," Dave answered, "and so may the governor of this province, who is skulking in yonder building. The governor and his followers may have secretly fomented this rebellion, in order to have a chance to loot the mission and secure, as they thought, the buried treasure which we know doesn't exist. And the governor, knowing how quick Uncle Sam would be to send a gunboat here, may have sent 'Burnt-face' to Manila to find some white rascal who could get acquainted on board the 'Castoga,' and perhaps thwart our plans. Pembroke may be here, even now, for the purpose of springing some treachery."

"That is an awful thought, Dave!" cried his wife.

"But it may be pretty close to the correct guess," Ensign Darrin rejoined. "At any rate, I shall have a pretty close watch kept on the movements of Mr. Pembroke!"

CHAPTER VIII—THE SWARM OF NIGHT FURIES

Late in the afternoon another meal was prepared.

Though the yamen was surrounded on all sides, and "sniping" was engaged in from time to time, the Chinese besiegers made no attempt to rush the compound.

Toward the end of the afternoon Dave carried on some vigorous signal talk with his commanding officer aboard the "Castoga."

"It does not look safe for you to risk bringing party through to river," came the message from the gunboat. "Do you think you can hold the yamen through the night?"

"Think I can hold yamen through the night," Dave signaled back, "if you sanction my using extreme measures at need. I may have to put the Chinese soldiers on the other side of the gate before dark comes on."

"Do so, if absolutely necessary," came the part approval. "If you wish, I will try to get thirty more men through to you. Cannot spare more without crippling ship."

"I believe so small a force as thirty men would be massacred in the streets before reaching here," Dave signaled back. "Would advise against your trying to send small reinforcements."

"Am trying by wireless," signaled the gunboat, "to pick up other naval vessel along the coast. If I establish such communication, will endeavor to have at least one hundred additional men sent up, even if they have to ascend river in motor launches. Think, if you can hold on until to-morrow, I can send substantial reinforcements."

"Will hold out through the night, if we have to keep shooting every minute," Darrin signaled his commanding officer.

"Have you plenty of ammunition?" came the query.

"Yes," Dick signaled back. "Have been firing cautiously."

Just before dark came on the gunboat signaled:

"Good luck through the night."

"Thank you," Ensign Dave caused to be signaled back.

After a conference with Dan and Bishop Whitlock, Dave decided upon bold measures. Toward every party of Chinese soldiers, on the ramparts or in the compound, went, all at once, small parties of sailors. In a twinkling, and almost without protest, the sailors seized the rifles of the yellow soldiery.

"Form the governor's troops in the compound," was the order that Darrin suddenly bawled forth.

"What are you about to do?" demanded Sin Foo, from the rampart.

"We are about to gag you, Mr. Sin Foo, if you open your mouth again," came the young ensign's stern answer.

Quickly the native troops were formed below. Dan, in the meantime, massed a strong force and two machine guns on the rampart over the main gate. At a signal the gates were thrown open. The blinking, unresponsive yellow soldiers were driven forth, and the gate shut fast on them. Dan's precautions overhead had been taken in case the armed multitude beyond should attempt a rush when the gate was opened. But Dave put through the whole maneuver successfully.

Leaving a guard of only seven men on a side, and massing his fifty-six other fighting men, Dave marched up to the governor's yamen.

"The move that I am going to take may bring down a torrent of official abuse upon my head," thought the young ensign.

First he called out a summons to open the door of the governor's dwelling. There being no answer, he directed several sailors, with a pole on their shoulders, as a battering ram, to smash in the door. Once the door was down, Dave led his party inside, and began searching from room to room.

At last he came upon the governor, surrounded by the same score of soldiers. In addition were "Burnt-face" and some dozen attendants.

41

"Disarm the soldiers," came Darrin's instant order, as he marched his command into the spacious, handsome, richly furnished room in which the governor had taken refuge. "Do it without fuss, if you can, but take the guns away."

Three of the soldiers attempted to resist, and were promptly knocked down by the sailors; after that, all submitted to disarming.

"March these yellow soldiers outside and give them the gate," smiled Ensign Dave. "Leave 'Burnt-face' and this servant with the governor, and put the rest of the attendants outside too. Forward, march!"

That audacious move was carried out without a hitch.

"Pass the word for Mr. Sin Foo," Dave ordered. Then, when the indignant under secretary appeared, Dave went on:

"Mr. Sin Foo, kindly assure his excellency that we have acted in the only way possible, and that we mean no harm to him, unless he should make such action necessary. Tell the governor that we have put his people outside because we do not intend to have any nonsense here to-night."

Sin Foo started to speak.

"Pardon me, Mr. Darrin," interposed a missionary, "but the under secretary is not interpreting correctly. He is abusing you to the governor."

"Look here, my friend," warned Dave, placing a heavy hand on Sin Foo's shoulder, "either you play fairly, or you will find yourself in more trouble than one poor under secretary can be expected to handle easily. Tell his excellency just what I said."

Governor Tai-pu listened in silence. Nor did he offer any comment when Sin Foo had ceased speaking.

"Does his excellency understand?" Dave asked.

"He does," replied Sin Foo.

"Yes," nodded the missionary who had interposed.

"His excellency will be required to remain in the open with us to-night," Darrin continued. "We must have him where we can easily keep both eyes on him."

"I beg your pardon, Mr. Darrin," said one of the missionaries, approaching. "Do you think it will be prudent to have lights in the compound to-night?"

"It will be much better to have them," Dave replied, "provided that no glow from them is reflected toward the ramparts. Any light behind our men, that showed them more distinctly to the enemy, would imperil our safety. But lights in one point at least in the grounds would be advantageous, as such illumination would tend to make the women less afraid. It's human nature, you know, sir, to be more afraid in the dark, and we must give every possible thought to the feelings of the women on such a trying night as I fear this is going to be."

Thanking him, the missionary hurried away, beckoning to three other men to follow him. These soon returned, bearing armfuls of Chinese paper lanterns. Cords were tied from tree to tree in the center of the compound, and from these lighted paper lanterns were soon dangling. In and out of the lighted area passed the women and other non-combatants, strolling about.

"That looks like a glimpse out of a pretty picture," said Dave, to his brother officer, as the two stood on the river side of the ramparts.

"Especially with the glow that the lanterns cast on a background of picturesque Chinese buildings," Danny Grin agreed. Then he turned to gaze into the darkness beyond, adding:

"David, little giant, we shall have very little to do with pretty pictures to-night. The nightmares of war will claim the greater part of our attention."

One group of women there was that did not appear. They comprised the women of the governor's family, who, with the children of the yamen, had taken refuge in one of the larger buildings. They were not required to come out into the open.

"Sir, I think I see figures advancing," whispered a sailor, gliding up to Ensign Darrin.

In an instant Dave threw up his night glass.

"You're right," he answered, in a low tone. "Pass the word to the men at the machine gun to be ready."

Stepping quickly down the little line on the river side of the wall Dave gave whispered instructions to the men to lie low and to await the order to fire.

Then, motionless as a tree, Darrin stood for fully two minutes, with the glass at his eyes.

"Ready!" he called, at last, in a low, but penetrating voice. "Aim! Fire!"

As the volley crashed out, Danny Grin raced around to the west rampart, to look for signs of a Chinese advance against that side.

Hundreds of Mongols had stolen forward on the river side. Instead of checking these, the brisk American fire brought thousands of others swarming from the streets and buildings.

"Keep that machine gun going," shouted Darrin in the ear of the machine gun captain. "Make it hot, my men! We want to get as many of the yellow fiends this time as possible. The more bloody they find this charge the more careful they will be through the rest of the night."

To add to the din Danny Grin had ordered the machine gun on the west side to fire, directing also his riflemen to fire only as sharpshooters.

Rightly judging that the attack on two sides might be only a feint to draw attention away from the biggest movement of all on the southern side, Darrin darted around to that point, traveling on the rampart.

Nor had he been there two minutes before the howls of thousands of infuriated yellow men sounded on the open ground before the wall.

"Pump that machine gun," Dave ordered sharply to the men at the gun. "Riflemen! Fire at will, and shoot as straight as you know how!"

This latter order he repeated as he darted along the line.

"Here, my friend, you get down! Lie behind the parapet; don't expose yourself in that fashion," Dave ordered, pushing down a sailor who had knelt on the parapet instead of lying behind it.

"I wanted to get a better aim, sir," replied the young sailorman, upturning a face full of enthusiasm.

"And you want to show your sand, too," nodded Dave appreciatively. "None doubts your courage, my man, but the fighting man who exposes himself needlessly draws just that much more fire toward comrades close to him. Remember that, and keep down."

Plunk! plunk! Dave was just in time to see the tops of two ladders planted against the stone ramparts by yellow men under the walls.

"Look out, men!" he yelled. "The Chinks are trying to plant ladders and scale the walls! Beat 'em back, or we are gone!"

A yellow face appeared at the top of one of the ladders. Like a flash Ensign Darrin bounded forward, bringing down his sword on the left shoulder of the yellow man.

Then, without a moment's further thought, Darrin seized the top of the ladder, giving it a mighty push that sent it toppling to the ground below. In a moment he had sent the second ladder, with three men on its rungs, after the first.

Drawing his revolver, and throwing himself across the parapet, Ensign Dave emptied ten shots into a mass of yellow humanity at the foot of the wall. Some of the sailors followed his example.

But now it seemed as though nothing would daunt the desperate, rat-like courage of the Mongols.

All along the four sides of the rampart, light bamboo ladders were set up. Hundreds of yellow assailants rushed up these ladders.

"Prepare to repel boarders!" lustily howled one sailorman, as he sprang forward, clubbing three Chinese in succession over the head.

But it looked as if the American force must be overwhelmed, for with fiendish fury the yellow swarms toiled up and fought at the edge of the parapets.

CHAPTER IX—THE TRAITOR OF THE YAMEN

How they ever came through the next fifteen minutes was afterwards a mystery to Dave and Dan.

They were in the thick of that frantic, deadly scramble for possession of the ramparts. As fast as Chinese assailants fell they were instantly replaced by others.

When Dave's revolver was not barking, his sword was in action, and his arms fairly ached with the labor of pushing away ladder after ladder. Hardly one of Dave's men was less occupied. Many of the Chinese had dropped the rifle for the long spear, or else for the keen, two-edged sword. American blood flowed in that quarter of an hour.

Boom! Out of the darkness came a trail of fire. Bang! A shell from the "Castoga" exploded among the nearest buildings on the river side beyond the yamen compound. In another moment flames were leaping upward from a flimsy house in which a shell had exploded.

Boom! Other shells began dropping about, on three sides of the compound. Soon a score of native houses were in flames, the light showing to the marksmen on the parapets just where to "find" their yellow assailants.

But no shell was fired over the yamen. Plainly the "Castoga's" gunners feared that they might drop a shell into the compound itself.

On three sides the flames of the conflagration made the surroundings nearly as bright as in daytime. The men on the ramparts could now see excellently, and aim accordingly.

At the same time the attack by ladders ceased, for now the laddermen were too plainly visible and could be killed with ease.

"Great work, that done by the shells!" chuckled Danny Grin.

"Yes," nodded Dave, "but I wish we could have the same kind of illumination to the southward. Withdraw enough men from the other three sides, Dan, to strengthen the southern rampart sufficiently."

The machine guns barking out anew, and with increased deadliness, the thousands of fanatical Chinese, now finding themselves too much in the spotlight, soon withdrew to a distance. From the darkness on the farther sides of the fires, however, they still kept up a sniping fire.

"Watch from the south wall, Dan," urged Ensign Darrin. "I'm going down into the compound to see how it fares with our wounded."

Throughout the deadly assault by the ladder men no American had been killed, but several had been wounded.

Many were the "jackies" who, binding handkerchiefs over their wounds, stubbornly remained at their posts.

In the circle of light under the paper lanterns, Dave found a medical missionary, assisted by some of the women, attending to the wounded.

Five sailors, two marines and three missionaries comprised the list of the more severely wounded. All were cheerful, however, and none seemed in danger from his wounds.

Not until Dave had gone the rounds did Belle step forward.

"Have you a moment to tell us anything?" she asked quietly.

"Yes," smiled Dave, resting an arm on her shoulder. "We are going to have quite a noisy night."

"Are you going to be able to hold the yamen against the Chinese?"

"That's exactly what we're here to do," answered Dave with a confident smile.

"But are you going to be able to do it?"

"Yes," the young ensign declared.

"You are not saying that solely to cheer us?" persisted Belle. "You are sure that you can hold out?"

"If there's any power in American fighting men, we can," Dave asserted.

"But you have ten men here who are out of the fight. How many more such losses can you stand?" Belle demanded calmly.

"If the 'Castoga' keeps on setting fires around us, I don't believe we shall have to stand many more losses," Dave assured her, and glanced past his wife at the other women who had gathered about them.

"Then," pursued Miss Chapin, taking up the questioning, "you don't consider that there is any likelihood of our being overwhelmed?"

"It is possible, but I firmly believe that we are going to be able to hold off the enemy all through the night," said Darrin. "The Chinese are attacking us in great numbers, and they are well armed and desperate. But we are all Americans on the walls, and there is a something in the morale and fighting fiber of an

American that bears down and overawes the Chinese. They have hurt ten of our men. I believe that we have put at least a thousand of the yellow men out of the fight. That is all I can say now. Is it enough to reassure you, ladies?"

"It is enough," spoke up another woman, "to make us thankful that we have American men, instead of men of any other nation to defend us in this night of terror."

Bowing to the women, Dave kissed Belle, then passed on. She did not seek to detain him; she was proud of her husband, confident of his fighting qualities, and aware that he could, at present, devote little time to her.

"The yellow men are creeping up again on this side, sir," called down the voice of a petty officer from the rampart that faced the river.

"When you think they're close enough, let 'em have it, and let 'em have it strong," Darrin called back. "Use the machine gun, but don't waste ammunition."

"Aye, aye, sir!"

Soon a pattering of shots on the north rampart announced that the yellow men were once more attempting to come in close. Dave did not rush at once to the top of the wall, for he knew, by the comparative lightness of the fire of his own men, that the attack had not become serious. The officers there were capable of handling the situation.

From the red glow against the sky. Ensign Darrin knew that some of the Chinese dwellings were still burning, giving ample light to enable his men to serve as sharpshooters.

"My heartfelt thanks are due for that bombardment by the 'Castoga,'" the young ensign told himself. "With light to shoot by we must score at least five times as many hits as would be possible without it."

Crossing to the southern side of the compound, Dave ascended nimbly to the rampart. Dan came forward to meet him.

"Nothing but a little sniping going on at present," reported Dalzell. "The nearest approach to trouble appears to be at the north side, facing the river. Shall I go back there?"

"I believe that this side will again witness the heaviest fighting," Ensign Dave rejoined. "You had better remain here."

Again Dave went below. Listening for a moment to the sounds of firing, he crossed the compound in no great haste. Past the circle of lighted lanterns he went. Had he not taken a second quick look at the main gate on the north side Darrin would not have noticed what was happening.

Starting violently, he looked again.

Yes, that big, double gate, moved by some unseen force, was swinging open. In another instant it would admit into the compound, the vanguard of a mob of frantic yellow men.

With a gasp of terror, when he thought of the defenceless women in the yamen Ensign Dave Darrin rushed forward at a run, revolver in hand.

CHAPTER X—THE CLIMAX OF THE ATTACK

As he ran in beyond the zone of light by the gate, Dave saw more clearly through the darkness. Good reason was there for that double barrier to swing open.

At the wheel and windlass of the gate stood Pembroke, both arms tugging hard and succeeding in slowly swinging the halves of the gate inward.

So intent was he upon his treacherous achievement that Pembroke neither saw nor heard the man dashing upon him.

Whack! A blow with the butt of Darrin's revolver laid the scoundrel flat.

On to the gate dashed Dave, just as an exultant yell outside told him that the yellow multitude was about to rush in.

Slam up against the gate rushed Ensign Dave, the force of his body sending the two halves shut.

Outside the tumult increased, as scores of yellow shoulders were hurled against the barrier.

"Help! Here! Quick!" roared Darrin.

Above the tumult his voice carried hardly any distance.

The pressure of the Chinese outside must finally overcome his straining muscles as he struggled to keep the gate closed.

Just then a sailor passed at a trot, with a message. Hearing Dave yelling for assistance, he looked at the gate and made out the figure of his officer there, trying to hold off the multitude.

"All hands to the gate!" yelled the seaman, using his hands as a trumpet. Some of those within the circle of lanterns heard, and took up the alarm.

Jackies rushed to Darrin's side, hurling themselves with all their strength against the gates. Their combined efforts seemed to be as nothing.

Three of the missionary party had hurried to the spot. There were now five men against the scores outside.

The mechanism of the gate had not been wholly opened, and that fact helped greatly.

Sailors and marines sprang up from many quarters. By this time, if the Chinese succeeded in getting through they would find themselves confronted by a platoon of rifles.

"Hold fast!" yelled Dave. "Ross, come with me!"

Officer and man rushed to the wheel that controlled the opening and closing of the gate. Seizing this, and throwing into it all their combined muscular force, they succeeded in driving the double barrier close.

"Here are the double bars!" shouted one of the marines at the gate. "Some one took them down."

Up went the bars, which were now made fast in place, and once more the gate was securely closed.

Placing a whistle to his lips, Dave ran along the wall. Even above the Babel of voices the shrill note of the whistle was heard.

"Aye, aye, sir!" bawled down a petty officer overhead.

"Turn your marksmen loose on that rabble before the gate. Use the machine gun, too. Make it as deadly for the scoundrels as you know how. Up to the ramparts you men at the gate, and fire on the mob!"

Chinese yells of battle changed to groans of pain as the American firing rattled out more heavily than at any other time that day.

From the river came the broad white beam of the "Castoga's" search light.

Boom! A shell dropped in the rear of the multitude and more houses were in flames, lighting up the scene.

"Hammer them as they run!" breathed Ensign Darrin fervently. "Keep it up as long as you can see any one to shoot at."

Boom! The "Castoga" took a further hand, by dropping one shrapnel shell, and then a second, among the seething, yellow rebels revealed by the searchlight.

Within two minutes the great open space had been cleared, save for the bodies of several hundred killed and wounded.

"The searchlight is sending a signal, sir," spoke up one of the men.

There on the rampart, Dave read these words as they were signaled in the code:

"Good work, Darrin and all hands!"

"Give our commanding officer three times three, and do it with a will!" shouted Ensign Dave. "Our shipmates will hear it."

And hear it they must have, for, no sooner had the cheering on the rampart ended when a distant, yet distinct sound of cheering drifted in from the river.

"How many have you on your casualty list?" was signaled by the searchlight.

"Seven of my men and three missionaries," answered the signal man, as he stood wigwagging, using a Chinese lantern hastily appropriated for that purpose. "None killed. All women safe."

Fast as he was with his wig-wagging, the signalman was glad when he had finished his work, for such a storm of bullets sang by him that none could understand how he escaped with his life.

Not until now did Darrin have time to think of Pembroke.

"I must get that blackguard!" he muttered, running down into the compound.

At first Dave could not locate the fellow. At last, however, he sighted him, half-hiding against a part of the wall where the gloom was most pronounced.

"Well, sir?" demanded the young officer, striding up to the man who held a handkerchief against his injured scalp.

"Was it you who struck me down?" demanded Pembroke.

"It was."

"Why did you do such a dastardly thing?"

"Das—" gasped Dave, astounded. "See here, fellow, don't you believe that I knew what you were up to?"

"I—I was trying to close the gate, which some of the scoundrels outside had partly succeeded in opening," Pembroke asserted stoutly.

"You lie!" retorted Ensign Darrin, staring sternly into the Englishman's eyes. "You were opening the gate. The direction in which you were swinging the wheel proved that. And I struck you down!"

"You are wronging me fearfully, Darrin!" Pembroke protested, with a strong attempt at injured dignity.

"Then I'm going to injure you still more outrageously," Darrin retorted, "for I'm going to place you in arrest. Moreover, if I live to get to the 'Castoga,' you are going out there with me as a prisoner."

"Darrin, you—you must be joking," stammered the fellow.

"No; I am not—Rogers!"

Dave watched for the effect of that shot. At mention of the name Pembroke turned more pallid.

"What do you mean by using that name when addressing me?" he stammered.

"Because it's your right name," Dave retorted. "You used that name before you ever used the name of Pembroke. Rogers, you are under arrest. Walk on ahead of me, straight to the circle of the lanterns. Don't attempt to trifle with me, for my patience was never so short as it is now. March!"

"Surely, you are not going to humiliate me before all the ladies," protested the prisoner. Warned by the light in Ensign Dave's eyes he started forward.

"That's exactly what I'm going to do," snapped Darrin. "I'm going to expose you so fully that you'll get no recognition save that of scorn."

"Darrin, one of these days you're going to pay a big penalty in regrets and apologies," the prisoner warned him.

"Fiddlesticks!" uttered Dave disgustedly.

Marching the fellow up under the light of the lanterns, Dave found several women eyeing him strangely.

"Why, is Mr. Pembroke a prisoner?" cried Lucy Chapin.

"He is, Miss Chapin," Dave assured her.

"But surely, he can have done noth—"

"All he did, Miss Chapin, was to try to open the main gate of the compound wall and let in the Chinese rabble. I caught him in the act, but, beyond knocking him down, I did not have time to attend further to him just then. On the fellow's head you will observe the cut made by the butt of my revolver when I struck him down."

"It seems so impossible to believe!" murmured Miss Chapin.

"And Mr. Pembroke, ladies, is also the rogue who once went under the name of Rogers. Further, I am convinced that this Pembroke, or Rogers, has been in league with the governor of Nu-ping, and with the governor's underlings. I am certain, in my own mind, that this fellow is largely responsible for the attack on the mission, and for all our troubles on this day and night."

Dave's plain words and his simple, straightforward manner carried conviction even to those who were, like Miss Chapin, reluctant to believe ill of the one who had called himself Pembroke.

"Marine, there!" called Dave, turning. The sea-soldier stepped over, saluting.

"You will take charge of this prisoner and be responsible for him. You will be prompt to shoot him if he tries to escape."

"Aye, aye, sir!"

Dave Darrin turned to lift his cap to the ladies, but started, turned, gasped.

In an instant such a din had arisen as he would once have believed could come only from the infernal regions.

From all four sides at once came the angry yells of thousands of men, mingled with thousands of detonations. The crashing racket of numberless gongs made the night still more hideous. The storm of noise was ear-splitting, nerve-racking.

Believing the south wall to be the place most in danger, Dave rushed across the compound in that direction.

CHAPTER XI—A SURPRISE PARTY FOR THE GOVERNOR

"It's Chinese war—*real* Chinese war!" roared Danny Grin in his chum's ear, as he pointed down at the packed throng in the open beyond the compound. "The heathen are beating gongs, ringing cowbells, shooting off firecrackers and yelling like wild-cats—just as the Chinese did in battle a thousand years ago. They're trying to scare us to death with their racket."

"It's awful to turn a machine gun loose on a tightly packed crowd like that," shivered Dave, "but you've got to do it. Turn it loose, Dan, and keep it going. I leave you in charge at this point."

Dave ran around the rampart to the western side. As he hastened he grinned at the Chinese idea that noise can play any big part in winning a battle. Yet even Darrin admitted that the din was abominable enough to shake the strongest nerves.

At the western wall he gave his orders, then rushed onward to the north wall, which included the main gate.

As he ran, he noted again a low, stone building which he had several times passed in the compound. The roof was not high, and suggested that it covered merely a cellar underneath.

Dan believed that, if the fanaticism of the approaching multitudes were to last a few minutes longer, the rabble would be able, despite the most desperate resistance by the Americans, to sweep up over the walls and massacre every white man and woman in the yamen.

"Why didn't I think of that before?" Darrin asked himself, looking down at the low-arched stone building. "That must be the governor's magazine. I wonder if it holds any ammunition?"

Descending at a run, Dave strode over to a place where, under a separate fringe of lighted lanterns, sat the governor of Nu-ping. At one side, eyes downcast, Sin Foo and "Burnt-face" sat.

"Mr. Sin Foo," Dave began, "that is a magazine over there, isn't it?"

Not glancing up, the under secretary addressed the governor in humble tones.

"Yes, it is a magazine," answered the under secretary, at last.

"Is there any powder stored there?"

Again Sin Foo addressed the governor.

"His excellency is not certain whether there is powder there or not," replied the interpreter.

"Hand me the key," commanded Dave. "I will look for myself."

At this there was more prolonged conversation between Sin Foo and his august though at present dejected chief.

"Hand me the key," Ensign Darrin insisted brusquely, "or I shall take other measures."

Only a few words passed in Chinese this time. Even that had to be shouted, for the clamor beyond the walls was indescribable, and the roar of machine guns and the rattle of navy rifles was all but deafening. Sin Foo, fumbling under his own long robes, produced a massive bronze key.

"Good enough," said Dave, "provided this be the right key." Then, turning to one of the sailors, who had come down into the compound on an errand Dave asked:

"You have an electric searchlight with you, haven't you?"

"Aye, aye, sir."

"Then come with me, on the jump."

Both hastened over to the low building that Dave had imagined to be the magazine. The key fitted, the lock yielded easily. Officer and man stepped inside.

"Powder!" gasped the sailorman. "Looks like two hundred kegs of it here, sir."

"Hand me the light and force open one of the barrels," Dave directed.

In a few moments the head of one of the barrels had been sprung. Taking a handful of powder outside, Dave placed it on a sheet of paper from one of his pockets, and touched a lighted match to one corner of the paper. When the traveling flame reached the powder there was a bright flash, accompanied by a puff of smoke.

"That powder is excellent," remarked Darrin.

"Aye, aye, sir," assented the seaman. "Are you thinking, sir, of using any of this stuff to plant among the heathen outside?"

"Only in case they succeed in getting into the compound," the young ensign replied, coolly. "I am going to ask the ladies if they prefer to group themselves around this building. Then, at the last moment, if all our forces are driven away from the ramparts, we can fall back on this magazine. When we see that the Chinese are bound to overwhelm us, a match dropped in a powder train here will save all of the women from Chinese torture. What do you think of the idea, Sampson?"

"All in the day's work for men of the Navy, and the best thing, I reckon, sir, for the ladies under the circumstances," answered the seaman.

"I believe that will be the general opinion," answered Dave. "Sampson, you know how to stack this thing so that a flash of light in a powder train will set off the whole magazine?"

"Aye, aye, sir."

"May I leave you here and depend upon you to fix the mine so that it will go up in the air at my order?"

"You may, sir."

"Thank you, Sampson," replied Dave Darrin, gripping the sailor's hand hard. "You're the right shade of blue, and a real man of the Navy."

"The same to yourself, sir, thank you," rejoined Sampson, taking back his electric lamp and going inside the magazine.

Dave ran over to the spot where the women had gathered.

"Ladies," he announced, gazing straight at each in turn, "I have an unpleasant announcement to make. From the look of things our men are presently going to be driven back from the ramparts. Then the yellow hordes will swarm over into this compound. If we are vanquished, have you any idea of the horrors of Chinese torture that will be inflicted upon you by the yellow fiends?"

Some of the older missionary women shuddered, turning their eyes heavenward, as though in agitated prayer.

"My wife is among you," Dave went on, speaking as softly as he could and make himself heard above the din of combat. "What I am going to offer you is the best, under the circumstances, that I can wish for her. That is—at the instant when hope must be finally abandoned—instant death. In the magazine there is a heavy stock of powder. One of my men is now laying a powder train which, when touched off, will explode the magazine. In my opinion, when all hope has gone, the wisest thing for all of you is to be near enough to die in the big upheaval of the exploding magazine. Do you agree with me that this will be the best step to take when there is no other hope of escaping from the Chinese furies?"

"Under such circumstances I will trust you to know what is best to be done," said Belle Darrin, resting a hand on her young husband's arm.

"Come, then," begged Dave. He led the way. By twos and threes the other women followed, though some of them faltered. The few men non-combatants removed the wounded to places near the magazine.

"Now," commanded Dave, turning to the marine who had just brought up the quaking Pembroke, "leave your prisoner here, and you and Sampson go and bring the governor and his attendants here."

When the governor and his little suite were brought to the magazine their faces betrayed unspeakable terror.

"May I ask what insane project is now being considered?" quaked Sin Foo.

"Certainly," Dave answered blithely in his ear. "When all other hope is gone, my fighting men will fall back to this spot. When we are all together, and your countrymen are about to conquer, we intend touching off the train of powder that shall blow us all free from Chinese vengeance."

Sin Foo turned several shades of frightened green, one after the other.

"Then you must liberate his excellency and his suite at once," cried the under secretary, falling forward upon his knees. "You cannot, you have no right to risk the governor of Nu-ping in such a fearful tragedy. Order your men to turn us free at once, that we may pass out through the gate!"

"Oh, no!" Ensign Dave Darrin retorted, with ironical cheeriness. "Your governor and his advisers are wholly responsible for the awful position in which we found our countrymen. For that reason His Excellency the August Governor of Nu-ping shall have the post of honor. He shall sit on top of the magazine, his suite with him!"

At a sign from Dave the governor was swiftly seized and boosted up on to the top of the arching stone roof. It was the first time that his excellency had been handled with anything like roughness. After his excellency Sin Foo and "Burnt-face" were almost tossed up after him.

The Governor Was Swiftly Seized.

"Let us down!" screamed Sin Foo piteously. "This is inhuman. Kill yourselves if you will, but you have no right to destroy us with you."

"If we go up in the air on the wave of a powder explosion, then your crowd goes, too," Dave roared back at him. "You shall have ample taste of the cake you have stirred for us all!"

Though his excellency, the governor understood no English, he appeared to have only too clear an idea of what was now going on. Howling, and nearly collapsing with terror, he endeavored to slip down from the roof of the magazine, but ready American hands thrust him back.

Sin Foo, too, made desperate efforts to slip down. As for "Burnt-face," that yellow scoundrel had fainted, and now lay prone on the roof.

"This outrage shall not be!" screamed Sin Foo.

"You'll soon know all about that," retorted Sampson gruffly, hurling the under secretary on his back on top of the magazine.

From the south rampart now came furious sounds of hand-to-hand conflict. Looking up, Dave Darrin saw that his own fighting men were all but surrounded by yellow fiends who had gained the rampart by means of ladders.

Pausing only a second to kiss his wife, Dave darted toward the nearest steps to that rampart, bounding up, sword in one hand, revolver in the other.

In the fleeting instant of turning after kissing his wife farewell, Darrin had shouted to Seaman Sampson:

"My man, I trust to your sand and judgment. Don't wait for my order, but fire the magazine trail the instant you think it is the only course left."

And after Dave had floated the sailor's cool, resolute:

"Aye, aye, sir."

CHAPTER XII—RISKING ALL ON ONE THROW

Just before Dave gained the parapet some of his sturdiest Jackies, by seizing a score of the yellow scoundrels and hurling them bodily over the wall on the heads of their countrymen below, had succeeded in clearing some elbow room in which to fight.

The machine gun at this point had ceased sputtering, for its server had been forced back in the rush.

Dave's sword flew in straight up and down cuts as he hurled himself among the furies who fought to drive him back. Thrice he parried spear thrusts that otherwise would have spitted him.

Rallying around him the strongest of his fighting men, Ensign Darrin drove the yellow men back for an instant.

"Tune up the machine gun," Dave bellowed. "We must rake this multitude again if we would have a single chance to win."

By signs, since he could not make himself heard many yards away, Darrin passed the word down the line for sailors and marines to fill the magazines of their rifles and fire into the Chinese, who were making an effort to raise new ladders against the wall.

But Ensign Dave glancing along his thin, exhausted line to see if many of them were hurt, muttered to himself:

"The next rush ought to sweep us down into the compound. Then for the magazine, and—the Big Noise!"

"Mr. Darrin," bawled a missionary from below, "your sailor, Sampson, ordered me to come to you to say that the governor is nearly dead with terror over his position. Sin Foo promises that if the governor be brought up here, his excellency will order and persuade the rabble to cease fighting and withdraw."

"Do you believe that, at this late stage, the governor could influence these thousands of mad men?" Dave demanded.

"It is more than possible," replied the missionary.

"Tell Sampson, if you please, to bring his excellency up here. If the governor makes one false move, back he goes to the top of the magazine, without any further chance to redeem himself from going up with the rest of us in the Big Noise. Please tell Sampson to rush the governor here."

"And shall I come back, that I may know just what his excellency says to the rabble?" suggested the missionary, who, like most of the others of his band, spoke the language of China.

"Be sure to come back, if you please," Dave begged.

Again swarms of ladders were rushed to the walls. Pigtailed heads were mixed with short-haired Chinese heads, for, though the republic desired all Chinamen to lop off the pigtails of the monarchial days, only a portion of the Chinese men have done so.

At times the swarms coming up the ladders pressed so close that sailors and marines fought them with the butts of their rifles and with fists, even. The superior athletic physique of the Anglo-Saxon bore up before the rushes of the Chinamen with seemingly tireless energy. Had the top of the rampart been broader the Chinese must have carried all before them, but in the narrowness of the top of the wall the sailors had the advantage.

Once more ladders had been tipped over, the last of the yellow men hurled to the ground below, and again the machine guns and the infantry rifles poured their shots into the thousands below.

Now up came Sampson, carrying in his arms a collapsed form that was the Governor of Nu-ping.

"Stand up, confound you!" adjured Seaman Sampson, planting the governor on his feet and seizing him by the collar. "Stand up!"

The greenness of the governor's yellow face was more ghastly than ever. He shivered as a few stray shots whistled uncomfortably close to his ears.

The rays of four pocket electric lights were turned upon him by as many sailors equipped with these articles. His excellency stood in the spot light, a very sorry-looking object.

Soldiers and civil officials are chosen from two different classes in China. Often these civil officials, when put to the test, prove to be timorous indeed.

"Tell him to secure silence and make his speech," Dave requested of the missionary.

His excellency's arms waved like a spectre's as he made gestures appealing for silence. Within thirty seconds the signs of his success with his own people began to appear.

Gradually motion stopped in the multitude. Some of the more lowly among the Chinese fighters, out beyond the thick of the rabble, even fell upon their knees.

The peril seemingly passed, the governor became steadier. He was a ruler speaking to obedient masses—or at least so it appeared.

Then, in a voice husky at first, but gradually gaining in strength, his excellency began to speak to his subjects, for such they really were. As his speech continued his voice became louder and more authoritative.

Dave glanced inquiringly at the missionary, who nodded back as much as to say that the governor was making a speech along right lines. Indeed, the speech must have had signal effect, for low murmurs ran in all directions through the lately fighting rabble, and by degrees the last efforts at fighting died out on all sides of the compound.

"As soon as the right moment comes," whispered Dave, "please tell him to order all the people a mile away from this part of the city."

In an undertone the missionary repeated in Chinese. Then, after a few moments, the movement backward began. A visible tremor of rearward motion passed through the throngs.

In silence the Chinese had heard the closing words of their governor, and now no crowd of thousands could have been more noiseless.

"Take his excellency below again," Dave commanded Sampson. "He is too valuable an asset to lose just yet. Put him on top of the powder magazine. Our missionary friends will assure his excellency that he is in not the least danger unless the attack is begun again."

Having seen these orders carried out, Ensign Darrin hurried back to the circle of lanterns.

"Ladies, I am glad to be able to say that I think our danger is nearly over," he announced. "We have a few more wounded to bring down from the walls. After these men have had attention I think we shall be ready to take up the march to the river, and soon after that I believe that you will all be safe on board the 'Castoga.' Don't rub your eyes or pinch yourselves to see if it all be true. I believe the bad dream is ended."

Then Dave sought out Sin Foo and "Burnt-face."

"Come with me to the governor," he directed, for, while the speech from the rampart was being made, these two underlings had somehow managed to slip away from their perilous place on top of the magazine.

"You are not going to offer us violence, are you?" asked Sin Foo fearfully.

"Not unless you do something to merit it," was Darrin's response. "I have other uses in view for you."

Securing the services of the same missionary, Dave directed him to ask the governor if he would trust Sin Foo and "Burnt-face" to go out into the city and carry to the people his excellency's will that no attack be made upon the Americans when they started for the river front.

The governor replied that his two secretaries were the very ones to carry his orders to his people.

"So that fellow is a secretary to the governor, also?" asked Darrin, pointing to "Burnt-face."

"He is the governor's secretary," replied the missionary. "Sin Foo is the under secretary, who, that he might deal with Englishmen and Americans, was educated in England."

"Warn the governor that if his secretaries play him false, and we are attacked, then his excellency will surely lose his life," Dave requested.

"His excellency is satisfied that his secretaries will serve him faithfully, and keep his life secure," the missionary declared.

The governor himself spoke to "Burnt-face" and Sin Foo, after which both bowed low.

"Now, you two may turn yourselves out into the street," Dave announced. "We will let you pass through the gates. See to it that you circulate well, and that you impress upon the people their governor's wishes. Otherwise, his excellency will sail sky-high on a keg of powder—you may be sure of that!"

To Ensign Dave's intense amazement, both "Burnt-face" and Sin Foo bowed very low before him. Next, they threw themselves upon their knees before the governor, who addressed them briefly, but earnestly.

When the secretaries rose Dave called a petty officer, to take them to the gate and to vouch for their right to pass out.

In the meantime the wounded were being attended. Nearly all of the unhurt defenders still remained upon the ramparts, though the great open spaces below were devoid of any signs of a hostile populace.

"I wonder if his excellency would like to change his shoes before starting," Dave suggested to Bishop Whitlock, as he glanced down at the governor's dainty embroidered silken footgear.

"Are you going to take the governor with us?" asked the Bishop.

"He must go with us to the river front, and must remain there until all of our party is safe," Darrin answered.

"But you really mustn't make him walk," objected the Bishop. "If you did, it would be such an affront as the people of Nu-ping would never forgive in foreigners. There are several sedan chairs in the yamen, and there are still enough attendants left to bear it. Permit me, Mr. Darrin, to see to the matter of the governor's sedan."

"I shall be deeply grateful, sir, if you will," was Dave's answer.

In less than five minutes the chair was ready, resting on the shoulders of eight husky coolies.

Ten minutes later the gates were thrown open. The defenders, hastily recalled from the ramparts, had formed.

First in the line were the marines, with a machine gun. Then followed a detachment of sailors. Danny Grin took command of the advance guard. Behind this were the wounded, some of whom hobbled slowly and painfully, as there was no conveyance except for those who had been badly hurt.

After the wounded came the women, in a body, and, behind them, the governor in his sedan chair.

There followed the missionaries, armed and unarmed, and the other male American residents of Nu-ping. Finally marched the rest of the seamen with Pembroke as their prisoner, and Dave commanded at this point.

Outside all was now as still as though in a city of the dead.

Was it safe to risk the march, or were they soon to run into some villainous trap prepared by the ingenuity of the Chinese?

"Forward, march!" Ensign Darrin sent the order down the line.

CHAPTER XIII—ALL ABOUT A CERTAIN BAD MAN

Like a long-drawn-out snail the procession crept through the yamen gates. The pace was set by the men most severely wounded.

Was it safe to leave the yamen while multitudes were yet abroad in the city, and those multitudes angry over the shedding of Chinese blood?

How many Chinese had fallen in the fight Darrin had no means of estimating. He had seen many fall, but dead and wounded alike had been promptly carried away by their own countrymen.

That the city of Nu-ping was in a ferment of anger there could be no doubt. Yet the governor, who had professed that morning to be unable to stem the revolution, had, by a few words, sent the fighting throngs back in the dead of night.

Last of all in the line walked Dave, in as uncomfortable a frame of mind as he had ever known. If his little party should be attacked and overwhelmed, and the women killed, he had made up his mind that he would make no effort to outlive the disaster. Death would be preferable.

There was still one other who knew less of comfort than any in the procession. That one was His Excellency, the Governor of Nu-ping.

In the sedan chair had been placed six kegs of powder, one of them opened. On top of the kegs, without as much as a cushion to soften the hardness of the seat, was his excellency, squatting, terror-stricken.

On either side marched a sailor with a loaded rifle. Also beside the sedan marched Sailorman Sampson, with a package of loose powder and a piece of slow-match found at the yamen. Seaman Sampson had his orders, with a considerable amount of discretionary power added, all of which was known to the governor with the greenish-yellow face.

As the line swung into the street on the way to the river, Danny Grin and two seamen trod softly ahead, alert for any surprises that might be met, particularly at street corners.

Not a sound was heard from natives, however, save for the occasional groans of the greenish-yellow governor, who, at that moment, was more fully posted on the feeling of absolute terror than was any other man in China.

No move was made on the part of the natives to stop the progress of the Americans. The party soon reached the wharf at the river front.

Now, with the women out on the wharf, Dalzell hastily drew up new lines of defense, pointing cityward, while Dave, with flashlight and whistle, managed to attract attention from the deck of the "Castoga" and to flash the signal to the watch officer.

It seemed but the work of a minute to get the launch and two ship's boats under way. The launch chugged busily shoreward. No time was wasted on explanations. The women and wounded were hurried into the boats and taken out to the gunboat.

On the next trip the rest of the party was speedily embarked.

As the last act, Sampson relaxed his watch over his excellency. Signs were made to the governor's chair bearers to take their lord back to the yamen. Nor did the departure of the governor take any time at all.

"Well done, Darrin! Fine, Dalzell!" boomed the hearty voice of Lieutenant-Commander Tuthill as the two young officers stepped on the deck of the gunboat. "Every man under your command has behaved like an American!"

Then, as his eye roved to Pembroke, standing under marine guard, he asked: "How came Mr. Pembroke to be in trouble?"

58

"Attempted treachery," Darrin responded. "I caught him trying to open the yamen gate to the Chinese rebels."

Tuthill's brow darkened.

"Pembroke, I did not think that of you, sir. You have a heavy burden of guilt! You will be taken down to the brig and locked up until I can decide what is to be done in your case, sir."

After Pembroke had been marched below, to go behind bars, the commander of the gunboat continued, in a low tone to Darrin:

"I am afraid not much of anything can be done with him. He is a British subject, I suppose, and guilty of an offense committed on Chinese soil. The most that I can do will be to keep him locked up until to-morrow, and then turn him loose. Perhaps the Chinese will take care of him. The ladies are waiting in the wardroom to thank Dalzell and yourself. You had both better go inside."

"I'd rather face the Chinese again," laughed Dan, "than have to stand and be thanked by a lot of women."

An hour later the ladies were established for the night, several of the officers' quarters having been given over to them. The American missionaries and civilians, like the sailors, were obliged to sleep in hammocks.

Just as Dave was seeking a mattress on the floor of the wardroom Surgeon Oliver hurried in. "Darrin," began the medical man, "did you know that Pembroke was badly hurt?"

"By the blow I gave him on the head?" queried the young ensign, wheeling.

"No, though that was quite bad enough. A stray bullet hit the fellow in the side, and he bound it up as best he could. He tells me that the shot hit him before you struck him down—perhaps an hour earlier."

"If I had known that," murmured Darrin, "he would have had somewhat softer handling."

"Pembroke is really in a bad way," continued the surgeon. "I have had him removed from the brig to the sick-bay, and have put a hospital attendant on watch over him to-night."

"Is he going to die?" asked Ensign Darrin.

"Can't say; I think not. But what brought me here is the fact that Pembroke asked if he might see you."

"Now?"

"Yes."

"Certainly."

Dave was tired out. Danny Grin was already sound asleep on a mattress on the floor. Darrin had been yawning heavily, but now the call of humanity appealed to him.

"I'll go with you, Doctor," Dave added, and followed the surgeon.

In a bunk down in the sick bay Pembroke tossed uneasily, his face a bright red.

"Here is Mr. Darrin, Pembroke," announced the medical officer.

"You'll think I had a jolly large amount of nerve to send for you," murmured the stricken man, holding out a hand. Under the circumstances Darrin did not hesitate to take the hand.

"Sit down, won't you?" begged Pembroke, and Dave occupied a stool alongside.

"I felt that I ought to see you," Pembroke went on. "Sawbones tells me I have plenty of chance to pull through, but I'm not so sure about that. If my carcass is to be heaved over in canvas, with a solid shot for weight, I want to go as clean as I can. So I want to tell you a few things about myself, Mr. Darrin. You don't mind, do you?"

"I shall be glad to hear whatever you have to say to me," Dave replied.

"You look jolly well tired out," observed the stricken man, "so I won't detain you long. To-night you accused me of being a scoundrel, and you had the goods on me. There can be no doubt about my being crooked, and I may as well admit it."

"Then you are really Rogers, instead of Pembroke?" Dave asked.

"I've used both names, but neither belongs to me. I have had so many names in my day that I barely remember my right one, which I'm not going to tell you, anyway. I came of decent people, and some of them are left. I'm not going to disgrace them. Darrin, I expect that I'm going to die, and I'm going to try to do it like a man—the first manly thing I've done in years. If I wanted to live at all now, it would be that I might stand and take my punishment for my connection with this Nu-ping affair."

"I don't believe that you could be punished for that by Americans," Dave went on. "You are a British subject, and your offense was committed on Chinese soil."

"I'm about as English as you are," returned Pembroke. "If I were a Britisher, and any good I'd been serving my country, right now, in France. I was born on the Atlantic seaboard of the United States. Out of decency I'm not going to name my birth state. At times, when it suited better, I've been an Englishman as a matter of convenience. But what I want to tell you about, especially, Darrin, is my connection with this Nu-ping business."

"Did that connection begin back in Manila?" Darrin asked.

"In Nu-ping first, but there was a Manila end. It won't take long to tell the story. I—"

In an instant a deadly pallor appeared in the stricken man's face. Then he lay silent.

"Doctor, I think Pembroke has gone," said Dave quietly, as he stepped over to the surgeon who was bent over another cot.

CHAPTER XIV—DAVE HEARS SOME EYE-OPENERS

"I'll look at the chap in a moment," replied Dr. Oliver.

But Pembroke had fainted, not died. Restoratives were applied, and presently he was ready to go on.

"Shall I listen to him now, or wait until to-morrow?" Dave asked the surgeon.

"The man will feel better if he talks himself out now," advised the surgeon.

So Dave sat down again, while Pembroke rambled on:

"You see, Darrin, this isn't the first time I have served Chinese officials among white men. I was in Nu-ping when that yarn got abroad that the missionaries had secretly looted that old temple and had removed millions in loot, burying the treasure secretly in the compound grounds of the mission at Nu-ping. You have no idea how such stories take hold in China. Doubtless, as a result of former rebellions and wars in China, the country is full of spots where fortunes have been buried for safety, with the people who buried the treasure killed off and the secret lost. I believed fully that the missionaries had buried such a treasure here at Nu-ping. The governor was sure of it, and so were his secretaries and the few other officials who had heard the story."

"Then why didn't the governor proceed officially and legally to have the mission grounds dug up and searched?" Dave asked.

"Don't you understand?" cried Pembroke. "If the governor had done that and found the treasure, he would have had to turn it over to the central government. In that there would be mighty little graft for his excellency. Now, unless he did it in an open and official manner, the missionaries could resist and report his excellency to the central government. Being a governor in China in these days isn't quite so fine a job as it was in the old days under the emperors. In those days the governor was called a viceroy—a ruler who served in the place of the monarch, and a mighty big chap a viceroy was. But these governors of the new breed are not such powerful chaps, though they still have many chances to steal without detection.

"But our yellow governor here at Nu-ping looked the situation over on all sides. He decided that it would be best to have a rebellion take place here on a small scale, have the missionaries killed or chased away, and then have his own men dig up the mission grounds and find the treasure. In the first place, our Nu-ping chap has about twelve thousand troops under his command. They could stop any rebellion that started around here. It was necessary to get the troops out of the way, so his excellency got ready to send them out of the way. He kept in town only the few troops you saw to-day. With so few soldiers he couldn't be expected to stop a rebellion, could he?

"The more his excellency thought over the matter of the hidden millions in the mission grounds, the more he itched for them. Sin Foo sent for me, and I talked it over with them. The rebellion, once started, might last quite a while. We looked over the American fleet in Asiatic waters and decided that the 'Castoga' was the only naval craft of light enough draft to come up the Nung-kiang River to this point. His excellency wanted to take time for a leisurely rebellion, but knew that this gunboat would be sent up here at the first murmurs of trouble. So he sent me to Manila to look over this craft, and, if possible, to cripple or sink her."

"Sink this gunboat?" asked Dave, in amazement.

"Yes," Pembroke nodded. "It struck his excellency as being worth while, in case his rebellion here should last long enough."

"But how could you sink the 'Castoga'?"

"Not such a difficult thing, if I got myself liked by the officers aboard," Pembroke replied. "Some afternoon I could put off and come aboard, carrying a suitcase. I could have asked you, or any other officer, to let me leave my case in his cabin over night, couldn't I?"

"Yes," Dave said. "But how sink the boat?"

"If the suitcase contained the right contents, and if those contents went off in the dead of night, it would be easy, wouldn't it?" asked Pembroke, flushing.

"And—you—you—would have done such a thing as that?" gasped Ensign Dave.

"I would have done it—at that time," Pembroke confessed. "Darrin, drifting through the Orient as I have done for some years, and always needing money—as I did—a fellow gets so he will do many things that he would hardly do in the good old home town."

Dave shuddered.

"His excellency's secretary—" Pembroke went on, but Darrin interrupted to ask:

"The 'Burnt-face' chap?"

"Yes. He went to Manila with me to see that I stuck to my job, and that I didn't misapply too much of the expense money that I carried."

"I want to ask you something, Pembroke," Dave broke in quietly. "Do you know anything about the Chinaman who was slain almost alongside this craft one night in Manila?"

"A good deal," the stricken man admitted. "He was a Christian convert, and the fellow overheard the secretary and myself talking of our plans. In trying to get away the eavesdropper made noise enough so that we pursued him. He escaped us, but we felt that he had to be found. Now, that Chinese convert, like most poor and simple people of his race, did not think of going to the police. He was bound to reason toward more direct procedure. My accomplice felt that the convert would try to warn the commander of the threatened gunboat. That was what he did. He put off alone, at night, to paddle out to the Castoga.' My accomplice and another Chinese pursued, and—well, you know what was done with the sword."

Dave looked up from a deep revery as Pembroke finished. As he did so he noticed that the surgeon and a hospital man had been listening in the shadow beyond. Witnesses to such a rehearsal were necessary, so Darrin did not object.

"But tell me one thing," Dave asked, presently. "In Manila I saw 'Burnt-face' look after Miss Chapin with a look amounting to hatred. Why should that have been?"

"Because, in the first place, the fellow hates all Christians, and missionaries in especial. Miss Chapin is a missionary; more, she is engaged to wed the Rev. Mr. Barstow, of the party that you rescued. Now, he and the Rev. Mr. Barstow have been at odds for some time, and the Chinaman hates the missionary most sincerely. Probably the secretary knew that Miss Chapin is engaged to Mr. Barstow."

"Why did you come up with the party with which Miss Chapin and my wife traveled?" asked Dave.

"Because it was the quickest way to get to Nu-ping," Pembroke admitted. "And my own reason for coming back here was to get my own share of the loot which, until to-day, I really believed existed in the mission grounds. Now, I think you know all. I—I--"

"You are very tired; I can see that," said Ensign Darrin quietly. "I am greatly obliged to you for what you have told me, for it has cleared up many points that had puzzled me."

"You think me a villain—an utter scoundrel, don't you?" asked Pembroke.

"Yes," Dave assented, speaking as quietly as before. "Any man who can plot to take innocent lives at wholesale is certainly a wicked scoundrel. But, if you should recover, I hope that you will lead a new life, and will be manly hereafter."

"I—I wonder if a man can do that, after he has led the kind of life that I have led?" smiled Pembroke, weakly.

"I think so. I believe that you can. But that is not as much in my line as some other questions. The man you should talk with is one of the missionary party. Shall I waken one of them and ask him to come to you?"

"Not to-night," Pembroke answered, tossing. "I am too weary. If I am alive in the morning, perhaps."

"Good night," said Dave, bending over the berth and holding out his hand.

"Can you shake hands with a fellow such as you now know me to be?" demanded Pembroke, in utter amazement.

"Not with the fellow you have been, but with the man I hope you're going to be," Dave answered. "Good night, Pembroke."

"Good night, Darrin."

CHAPTER XV—WHEN THE FLAGSHIP WAS SIGHTED

In the morning, when Darrin and his chum came on deck, the sun was shining brightly over Nu-ping.

Perhaps a hundred of the smaller houses of the place had been burned by the fires started by the gunboat's shells the night before, but in a whole city full of small Chinese houses the loss was not especially noticeable.

"You wouldn't want to land over yonder to-day, Darrin," smiled Lieutenant Warden, when Ensign Dave saluted him on deck.

"Why not, sir?"

"Soon after daylight the governor's troops marched into the city. As nearly as we could estimate the strength of the force from this deck, there are about twelve thousand of the troops, and with them are three batteries of field artillery."

"Are the batteries strong enough to be used against this craft?"

"The batteries might be able to give us a good bit of trouble to handle, but there is no danger of their being employed. It would cost the governor his head to turn his troops against us, for that would be an official act of his, and a violation of China's peace with us. Of course the pretended riot and rebellion of the populace was carried out by the governor's secret orders, but we could never prove that. His excellency will be questioned by the Chinese government, but he can claim that the rebellion started when his troops were in another part of the province. The governor will promise Pekin to punish the ringleaders of the rebellion. He will then proceed to 'try' and behead a few of his political enemies, and Pekin will be satisfied. That will close the incident."

A messenger came briskly up, with word calling the executive officer into the presence of his commander.

Pembroke's confession, which Dave and the witnesses had promptly reported to the Lieutenant-Commander the night before, was the talk of the officers this morning.

The wounded man was said to be in somewhat better condition. All of the wounded sailors, marines and civilians were reported as being in no danger of dying from the injuries received in the spirited fighting of the day before.

Dave's eyes caught sight of Belle the instant she stepped on deck. He hurried to her, looking her over closely to see how she had stood the excitement and terrors of the day before.

"Do you think I shall ever be able to qualify as a naval man's wife?" Belle asked, laughing.

"You won't have to qualify," Dave assured her. "You've already passed all the necessary tests."

"There were times yesterday when I was dreadfully afraid," shuddered Belle.

"Then you have mastered the necessary secret of how to conceal your fears," Darrin assured her. "There was many a time yesterday when I, too, was badly scared."

"You?" cried Belle, gazing at her husband, in astonishment.

"Yes," smiled Dave. "Did I betray myself?"

"You are jesting," Belle declared. "I saw you often, in the worst of the fighting and your courage and endurance were magnificent. Not once did you show any sign of faltering."

"None the less, I had my moments of scare," Darrin assured her.

"You surely *are* jesting," asserted Belle.

"Not a bit of it, my dear. Every man who has to fight and who is honest about it will admit that he is often badly scared."

"Am I interrupting a private conversation, Mr. Darrin?" asked the executive officer.

"Not in the least, sir," replied the young ensign, raising his cap.

"Then what I have to tell you is that our wireless picked up the admiral's flagship a little while ago, and we have reported what took place here yesterday. We are under orders to sail as promptly as possible, and the flagship will meet us at the mouth of the river. The flagship will also try to pick up some coasting steamer, which will carry the missionary party and others down the coast to Shanghai, which is considered a safer place at present for Americans."

"Did the Admiral approve of what was done here yesterday, sir?"

"He expressed neither approval nor criticism, but will take our detailed report when we join. The ladies will be summoned to breakfast soon, Mr. Darrin. Most of the officers will breakfast at second table to-day, but on account of Mrs. Darrin's presence on board you will go to first table with her. You will take my place at the head of the table."

"And, of course, as soon as the civilians are transferred to that coasting steamer I shall have to go with them," pouted Belle. "It may be months before I shall see you again. I had hoped to be with you at least a few weeks in Manila. Instead, I had to come here. I have had a day with you—and what a day!"

"It's hard, dear," sighed Dave, "but such is a naval officer's life. However, our turn will come. One of these days I shall be ordered to shore duty for a while, and then we shall be together, month after month. We shall even be able to have a little home of our own. It may be, dear, that my shore duty will be at Washington."

"Yes," groaned Mrs. Darrin. "And if you send for me to come and join you in Washington, by the time I arrive there I shall find out that you have just been sent away on a three-year rescue cruise to find some lost explorer at the South Pole! That is the Navy!"

When the breakfast call came Dave led his wife into the wardroom, conducting her to her seat at table and seating himself beside her.

Before the meal was ten minutes under way the deck watch began to make active preparations for the start down the river. As the anchor was being hoisted a large boat put out from the shore flying the governor's banner.

As it came alongside a great bale was hoisted on board, addressed, simply, "To the American Ladies."

An envelope bearing a similar address was brought aboard by an officer from the governor's yamen, as well as a second envelope addressed to Lieutenant-Commander Tuthill.

The second letter was delivered at once. It contained an expression of the governor's "profound regret" over the occurrences of the day before, and stated that, the governor's troops having fortunately returned, his excellency was now able to guarantee the safety of all Americans who might condescend to honor the city by their presence ashore.

The governor's letter ended with the statement that he had endeavored to express his apologies to the American ladies in a more tangible if very humble and poor form.

The American commander immediately dictated a letter thanking his excellency for his letter and assurances, but adding that, under orders, the American party was being taken to the mouth of the Nung-kiang River.

"Get this letter over the side and signal the engine-room for half-speed ahead," Lieutenant-Commander Tuthill brusquely directed.

So, before breakfast was ended, the "Castoga" was steaming down the muddy river.

Not until the officers and male guests had been served at second table was any mention of the bale made by the busy executive officer. Then the ladies were once more summoned to the wardroom, while two sailors undid the package that had come from the governor.

The contents would have made a gift fit, indeed, for a royal family. There were more than enough handsome furs to go all around. There were silks, such as are never seen in America. Gold hair ornaments and rare jade jewelry were there in abundance, and many other articles dear to the feminine heart.

"If this is a true expression of the governor's regret, then I wonder that he could ever have permitted the rioting to start," said one of the women.

"But, under the circumstances, have we any right to accept such valuable gifts?" asked Belle Darrin.

"Shall I have them thrown overboard, then?" queried Mr. Warden, smilingly.

"No; of course not," replied another woman, "but I feel that these magnificent gifts should be returned."

"How?" asked the executive officer. "This gunboat may never enter the Nung-kiang River again."

"It begins to look," laughed Dave, "as though the necessities of the case compel the acceptance of these visible expressions of the governor's invisible regrets. There is no way to send the stuff back."

It took an hour's discussion to convince the women that they must perforce accept. That point settled, they proceeded to divide the gifts by lot.

"Where am I going to put all this plunder?" Belle asked her husband as she gathered up her own considerable share of the "expressions of regret." "I haven't a single piece of baggage."

"I fear I shall have to place them in my chest, and turn them over to you when we next meet," Dave suggested.

"And I may very likely be an old woman by that time," sighed Belle.

At noon Dave took the bridge until four o'clock. It was just before his watch was finished that the mouth of the river was made. Two miles off shore the flagship could be seen, steaming back and forth. A quarter of a mile away a small ocean-going steamer followed a similar course.

"And I won't have a chance to cry on my husband's shoulder for a few moments," Belle complained, tragically, to another woman. "He's stuck away up forward on the bridge."

"Your husband will be off duty in ten minutes," Lieutenant Warden assured her. "He will have command of the launch that transfers the party to the coasting vessel."

"In the Navy the smallest favors look like great ones," Belle observed to herself.

Watch changed just before the gunboat ran up behind the stern of the flagship.

Relieved of his duty on the bridge, Dave received his further orders and immediately called the launch crew to quarters.

Launched and brought alongside, the motor boat was quickly filled with the refugees.

Dave gave the order to cast off, then sat down beside Belle. Their time was altogether too short. The halted coasting steamer received the refugees on board, Dave, too, going up over the side.

In the instant that he and Belle clung together she whispered:

"Shall I go to Yokohama and await the chance to join you?"

"That will be a fine idea, little girl!" cried Dave. Then with a final kiss he went down over the side and into the launch.

"Cast off. Make back to the gunboat."

The coastwise steamer was already sounding her hoarse whistle, and moving under slow way.

Once in the launch, Ensign Darrin stood up and waved his cap at the lonely little figure standing by the stern rail on the after-deck of the steamship.

Until the launch rounded up under the "Castoga's" quarter Dave waved his cap frequently. Through the mist that lay over his eyes he could barely see the answering fluttering of white on the deck of the southbound steamship.

"Let the crew remain in the launch," came from the officer of the deck. "Ensign Darrin will report to the executive officer."

"Lieutenant-Commander Tuthill and Ensigns Darrin and Dalzell are ordered aboard the flagship," announced the executive officer. "Mr. Darrin, you will make the necessary change in uniform."

Hastening to his quarters, Dave changed to full dress uniform for which the regulations now called. He girded on his dress belt, with his dress sword, and drew on white gloves. Then he gained the deck, saluting and reporting to the commander of the gunboat.

"We shall be called upon to make our report, Mr. Darrin, of the Nu-ping affair. It is a good thing that we can do so with clear consciences," smiled the Lieutenant-Commander.

"The Admiral may not approve of all that I did to His Excellency, the Governor," remarked Ensign Dave.

"I think he will," replied the commanding officer. "In my opinion, at least, you made the best possible use of your discretion."

"Thank you, sir."

Soon the three officers from the gunboat found themselves on the quarter-deck of the battleship "Katahdin," flagship of the Asiatic Fleet.

Captain Tucker received them and then remarked:

"I have orders to conduct you at once to Admiral Branch."

The Admiral gave the three visiting officers pleasant if formal greeting.

"This is my report, sir, in writing, of the affair at Nu-ping," declared Lieutenant-Commander Tuthill, passing over a bulky official envelope.

"Quite so," observed Admiral Branch. "I will read it at once."

For more than five minutes the three officers remained seated, and in silence, while the Admiral slowly turned the pages of the report.

From time to time the fleet commander frowned. Dave, noting this, wondered to what features of his conduct in Nu-ping Admiral Branch most objected.

"Dave is surely going to catch it," reflected Dan Dalzell uneasily. "I wonder if I shall come in for some of the scotching, too. But probably there'll be no such luck. Dave was ranking officer ashore, and I acted only on his orders. I wish I could take my share in the storm."

Having read the last page of the report, the Admiral slowly, thoughtfully folded it, laying it away in a pigeon-hole over his desk.

"Surely, Mr. Darrin, you found some new ways of treating a Chinese viceroy, or, I should say, governor," remarked the fleet commander dryly.

"I tried, sir, not to subject him to any annoyance or indignity that could be avoided," Darrin responded gravely.

"And in a way that would have been impossible, had the governor been attended by his usual number of troops," continued Admiral Branch. "Under the circumstances, however, you treated him in a way that I, as a junior officer, often longed to handle many an important Chinese official."

Though the fleet commander spoke gravely there was an unmistakable twinkle in his eyes. Dave's hopes began to rise.

"I shall endorse Lieutenant-Commander Tuthill's report as being satisfactory to myself," continued the Admiral, "and then shall send the report on through the usual channels. And I sincerely trust, Mr. Darrin, that the Navy and State Departments at Washington will also endorse the report. For myself, Ensign Darrin, I congratulate you on your handling of a most unusual and highly difficult lot of problems. I congratulate you, sir," continued Admiral Branch. "I shall be glad to have you aboard this ship."

"On this ship, sir?" asked Darrin, as he took the Admiral's outstretched hand.

"Yes; but that is another story, and perhaps I had better tell that first. Some transfers have been ordered in the Asiatic Fleet. Among other changes, Ensigns Holton and Brown, now on this ship, are ordered to duty on the 'Castoga,' and Ensigns Darrin and Dalzell are ordered to the 'Katahdin.' I fancy, gentlemen," turning to the two younger officers present, "that very likely you have seen as much as you wish of China for the present, so you will be glad to know that this ship is ordered to Japan, and that we shall likely be there for two months or more. You will move your baggage over to this ship and report for duty as quickly as possible."

CHAPTER XVI—THE MEDALLION MYSTERY

"Hullo, Darrin; come over here just a moment. I want you to see something that is rather unusual, even in Japan."

Two young men, who had just entered the American Club in Tokio, turned when this hail to one of them was heard.

The hail came from a group in which sat four Americans, one Englishman and three young Japanese. The latter three were in the uniforms of lieutenants of the Emperor's infantry.

"Come over with me, Dan," urged Dave in a low voice, as Dalzell held back slightly.

"I wasn't invited," murmured Dan.

"You simpleton, that's because Carter doesn't know you. I can introduce you, and that will set you straight."

"How are you, Carter?" asked Dave, as he went straight up to the young man who had hailed him and held out his hand. "I wish to introduce my friend, Mr. Dalzell, same service and same ship." In turn Dave and Dan were presented to all in the group.

The American naval officers wore blue civilian suits. Carter belonged to the diplomatic service, and was now stationed in Tokio. Dave had first met him in Washington. One of the other Americans was in business in Tokio, and the other two were tourists.

"Mr. Katura was showing us something so wonderful," Carter explained, "that I asked his permission to call you over to see it. Will you show that wonderful medallion again, Katura?"

The little lieutenant, who appeared to be very shy and diffident, flushed slightly as he bowed. Then, from an inner pocket, he drew out a small lacquer box, from which he took out and passed to Dave a filigree gold plate on which appeared the delicately tinted face of a beautiful Japanese woman.

"I never saw anything so wonderfully exquisite," gasped Darrin, in genuine admiration. "I didn't know that such beautiful work could be done."

"No one in Japan could do it to-day," spoke up another of the Japanese officers, Toruma by name. "That medallion comes from the most brilliant period of Satsuma art."

In that face the paler flesh tints had been laid, with wonderful minuteness of detail, from flawless mother of pearl. The hair, which stood out in life-like accuracy, had been worked in some highly polished blue-black stone. The teeth, as they showed in the parted lips of that tiny miniature, were real seed pearls, worked in the exact shapes of the teeth represented.

The most striking feature of all was the beautiful red lips of the tiny mouth. This red had been laid in fine rubies, not showing separately, but blended delightfully.

For fully two minutes Darrin gazed at the miniature face, fascinated with the beauty of the thing. Dan, standing by, admired it also.

"Now, try the effect of this magnifying glass on the face," suggested Carter.

"It would be almost wicked to hold a magnifying glass over such a treasure," protested Ensign Dave, recoiling slightly, as though from a profanation of an art treasure.

"Try the glass; don't be afraid," said Carter.

So Dave took the glass, focusing it over the wonderful medallion. A cry of wonder escaped the young ensign's lips.

"Can you find the slightest appearance of roughness under the glass?" asked the American diplomat.

"I cannot," Dave confessed.

"Think of the wonderful work of the artist," suggested Toruma, "who, in an age when magnifying glasses were unknown, could join all the parts of that inlaying so perfectly."

"It is wonderful," murmured Dave. "The artist's eyes must have been as keen as any magnifying lens."

For some minutes more Darrin examined the medallion, both with the glass and without. The Japanese, smiling and affable, stood enjoying his very evident pleasure. Their hearts warmed to a foreigner who could feel such real appreciation of the marvels of the ancient art of their country.

"Here, I am afraid that you had better take this from me," begged Darrin laughingly, at last. "If it is much longer in my possession I shall be under a temptation to commit grand larceny."

Smiling, Lieutenant Katura held out his hand to receive the treasure.

"It has been in our family for at least six hundred years," he explained proudly, though without any sign of boastfulness. "It belongs to my mother."

"I should think you would be afraid of its being stolen," suggested Dave.

"Ordinarily it is kept in the Okugawa Bank, in our family vault," explained the little lieutenant. "Once Mr. Carter saw the medallion, at our home, and to-day he begged me to bring it here to show to some of his friends. I am glad to have been honored with an opportunity to give you pleasure by the sight of it."

"But surely you don't carry such a treasure loosely in your pocket like that," Dave almost protested.

"Why not?" smiled Katura.

"Are you not afraid of its being stolen?" Darrin went on.

"Not likely," declared the little lieutenant. "I am able to defend myself, and I shall have my friends with me on my trip back to the Okugawa Bank."

"But pickpockets might brush against you in a crowd, and take it from you," Dave hinted.

"They will not have that chance," smiled Katura. "From here to the bank my friends and I will go in jinrikishas."

As the tiffin (luncheon) hour drew near, the club rooms began to fill. There were, perhaps, a hundred newcomers.

"You'll come to our table, Darrin?" asked Mr. Carter.

"I thank you, and under any other circumstances I would," Dave answered. "My wife will be expecting me at the hotel. She and I have not had many opportunities to lunch together since I entered the service. So I shall have to be going along soon."

"You'll stay, Dalzell?" asked the diplomat.

Dan decided that he would. The Japanese officers were invited to remain, but replied that they had duties claiming their attention.

So Dave left with Lieutenants Katura, Toruma and Hata. In the main corridor these departing ones found themselves somewhat delayed, owing to the press of the crowd about one of the coat-rooms.

At last they got through. A Japanese attendant, saluting the three officers of his own country, ran nimbly to the end of the porch, striking his hands together and summoning three jinrikisha men, who raced up to the steps.

"Farewell, for an hour or two, at least, American brother in arms," cried Toruma, the most talkative of the three Japanese. Friendly salutes were exchanged, and the Japanese trio were rushed away.

Dave's jinrikisha came around. In appearance it was an exaggerated baby-carriage, with shafts, between which a stout Japanese coolie played the part of a horse.

These curious little street vehicles are comfortable, and the seasoned coolie in the shafts often displays great speed. The slowest he is allowed to travel on short journeys, when he has a fare in his 'riksha, is five miles an hour.

"To the Imperial Hotel," said Dave briefly. That was all that was needed. The human "horse" in the shafts would do the rest.

In a few minutes Dave arrived at the big, handsome Imperial Hotel. This hostelry, famous among travelers in the East, is an imposing white pile, built originally by the Japanese government, that travelers might be sure of having a stopping place as comfortable as any in the lands from which they came. Bit by bit the management bought over the government's interest in the hotel, until now it is privately owned, though the pride of the Japanese is such that the government still supervises the hotel, and sees to it that the high standard is kept up.

As Dave Darrin entered he passed into one of the parlors at the entrance. Belle rose and came forward, a glad little cry on her lips.

"How thankful I am that I thought of coming to Yokohama!" she cried. "It was but a step to Tokio. And you are punctual."

"It is one of the virtues—or vices—of an officer and a gentleman," Darrin laughed, as he bent over to kiss her.

"And now are you ready for tiffin, dear?"

"I shall be as soon as I have made my toilet," Dave replied. "May I have your indulgence that long?"

"Certainly."

Going below Ensign Darrin washed off the dust of his forenoon's wanderings, smoothed back his hair, and with a final look in the glass drew on his coat and started above.

Dave was now in about the middle of a three-weeks' leave, which Dalzell had taken at the same time. In the Navy service an officer does not have, regularly, one day in every seven on which he is free from toil. He is on duty, day and night, seven days a week. By way of leisure he is allowed a certain portion of every month, when practicable, in the way of "leave." When an officer has no especial use for leave, he often allows it to accumulate, and then later on secures a long enough leave to use up his privileges in the way of absence from duty. So Dave was now on a three-weeks' leave—a "vacation" it would be called in civil life.

Several other officers from the "Katahdin" were in either Yokohama or Tokio. The former city, only a few miles from the latter, is the port of entry for the Japanese capital. In the harbor at Yokohama the American flagship now lay.

Up to the present Darrin had devoted most of his waking time to escorting Belle through the bewildering Japanese shops, to Uyeno Park, to the Japanese theatres, to the famous temples, and all the other sights that attract tourists.

But this forenoon Darrin had spent in going about Tokio, meeting a few of the people whom he had known in other parts of the world. There was Lieutenant Anstey, one of Dick Prescott's West Point chums, now on duty at the American Embassy; there were naval officers, and two or three men in the diplomatic service. Dave had even called at the Japanese Navy Department to shake hands with two Japanese officers whom he had met in Europe. These latter two were absent, and Dave, leaving cards, had promised to return in the afternoon.

"You are going to be busy this afternoon?" Belle asked as they sat at tiffin.

"I shall have to make two or three calls, but I shall come back to you as early as I can."

Two or three times it was on the tip of Darrin's tongue to tell his wife of the wonderful medallion he had seen that morning. In each case some remark or question of Mrs. Darrin's had prevented.

In the meantime, Lieutenant Katura, on entering the Okugawa Bank, had made an amazing and frightful discovery. The lacquer box, containing the priceless

Satsuma medallion, was not in any of his pockets! The young lieutenant's grief was most frantic. In vain Toruma and Hata tried to comfort him.

An hour after Ensign Darrin had left the Imperial Hotel, on his way to the Navy Department and elsewhere, Belle Darrin, going up to their rooms, found a little package and a note lying on a table in the middle of their parlor.

Scenting some loving surprise from her husband, Belle, womanlike, opened the package first, disclosing a small lacquer box. In the box she found the same medallion that had so fascinated her young husband that forenoon.

"Oh, oh, oh!" cried the delighted girl, in as many notes of happiness.

Then, still eager, she laid down the medallion and tore open the envelope. On a sheet of heavy paper she read:

"Dear Mrs. Darrin: This comes to your hand from one who is a stranger to you, but who is a most devoted friend of your husband. He has admired the pretty trinket which comes with this note, and I know that he had it in mind that he would dearly love to hand it to you. I am taking the liberty, as your husband's friend, of pleasing Ensign Darrin, the dearest fellow in the world. But I am going to ask of you a very unusual favor. Fearing that your husband might have the extreme delicacy to insist upon returning this bauble, I am going to ask you not to mention receipt of it until to-morrow. By that time the sender, as your husband will know, will be too far away for the immediate return of this trifle. By the time that he can communicate with me again I trust that he will have agreed to give me the great pleasure of making him happier through the knowledge that his wife possesses a treasure that I know he wished to secure for her.

With every best assurance,
(Signed) X. Polemkin."

This strange note dropped from Belle's fingers to the table. There was a clouded look in her eyes. She did not even turn for another glance at the priceless medallion.

"Secrets from my husband?" she murmured, pouting. "I don't believe I can do a thing like that. No; it wouldn't be right. As soon as Dave returns I must show him this medallion and the note."

Perhaps, in her heart, Belle hoped that Dave would tell her that circumstances were such that she might properly keep the gift so strangely sent. Be that as it might, Belle Darrin had no notion of keeping any secret that might mean a wound to her gallant young husband's trusting heart.

"I shall see what Dave says," murmured Belle, as she turned away from the table.

CHAPTER XVII—DAVE FACES THE HUMAN TEMPEST

Lieutenant Katura stood in the long counting-room of the Okugawa Bank, a film of despair over his eyes, while Toruma and Hata, their words exhausted, looked on helplessly. Just then a young man, perhaps an American, well-dressed, keen, hustling and alert, bustled up to them.

"Will you pardon my addressing you?" he asked. "I was at the American Club, and from the look on your face, sir, I fear that you may have been made the butt of too rough a piece of work."

"What do you mean, sir?" hastily asked Lieutenant Toruma, for Katura seemed incapable of speaking.

"Why, I saw you three on your way out through the crush around the coat room," explained the stranger. "With you was one of my countrymen, I should judge."

"An American, yes," Toruma nodded.

"I saw him play a little trick on your friend here," nodding at Katura. "At the time I did not think much about it, and I might have forgotten it, had not business brought me here. But my first look at you made me feel certain that something was wrong."

"Something *is* wrong," replied Lieutenant Toruma quickly. "But what was it that you saw near the coat room of the American Club?"

"I saw my countryman slip his hand in one of your pockets, sir," continued the stranger, addressing Katura. "He took out some small object—a lacquer box, I should say, but I cannot be sure."

"It *was* a lacquer box!" cried Katura, a fierce light leaping to his eyes, while his face, first paling, next turned to a deep red hue. "It is a lacquer box that I have just missed."

"And Mr. Darrin remarked that he felt much tempted to steal it," broke in Lieutenant Hata.

"Be still, Hata, please," begged Katura, recovering his own dignity. "Mr. Darrin is an American officer and a gentleman, not a thief!"

"I trust I haven't intruded, and that I haven't made any trouble," the stranger went on, hastily, "but you appeared to me to be in so much trouble that, as a gentleman, I felt I must speak to you."

"And I thank you from the bottom of my heart, sir!" cried Katura, his eyes once more gleaming fiercely, despite the gentleness of his words.

"It was probably all a joke," the stranger smiled, "but I am glad if I have been able to save you from any anguish of mind. Of course you will see my countryman—Barron, did you say his name is? I know that I may rely upon you all not to bring me into the matter."

"You may depend upon us for the courtesy that is due to one gentleman from others," promised Lieutenant Toruma.

Then, as their informant left them, the three Japanese held swift, sorrowful conference.

"Of course we must go to the hotel at once and see Mr. Darrin," proposed Toruma.

"I feel that it will be necessary," bowed Katura. "But let none of my friends suspect that it was more than a joke. An American officer and gentleman could not be an intentional thief."

"Even as a joke it was in very, very bad taste," declared Lieutenant Hata slowly and gravely.

"Say not so," urged Katura. "Let us say nothing, and suspect or accuse no gentleman."

"But let us go to the Imperial Hotel as fast as possible," urged Lieutenant Toruma.

"By all means," agreed Hata.

So Katura, who was sorrowful and dazed, felt thankful that he had loyal friends with him to do his thinking for him at this moment.

Not many minutes were needed for reaching the Imperial. Three little Japanese officers, with smiling faces, entered and went to the desk in the hotel office.

"We desire to see Mr. Darrin of the American Navy," declared Toruma, speaking in Japanese to the clerk, who was a fellow-countryman.

"I regret much to say that Mr. Darrin is out," replied the clerk.

"Then may we do ourselves the honor of waiting until your guest returns?" asked Hata.

"Officers of his majesty the Emperor will confer distinction upon this poor hotel by deigning to wait," replied the clerk.

So the three Japanese officers walked into a parlor, where they took seats, knowing that they would be notified when Ensign Darrin reappeared at the hotel.

At about this time, Belle, who had been absent from her rooms for a few moments, was looking diligently for the note that had accompanied the lacquer box.

"I closed and locked the door when I went out, so I can't understand what has happened to that note," mused Belle Darrin perplexedly, as she hunted about the room.

The medallion itself still lay on the table, but to that the young wife now paid no heed.

So much did the disappearance of the note perplex her that Belle spent some minutes in the vain search for it.

At last, a perplexed frown on her face, she again picked up the lacquer box and stood gazing at the exquisite, precious medallion.

Below, Dave entered the hotel. He passed quickly through, going to the stairs.

Not immediately did he go to his apartment. First of all he turned down a corridor on the second floor to speak to Lieutenant Barbes from the "Katahdin."

But the clerk, who saw Dave pass through the lobby, himself stepped into the parlor where the three Japanese lieutenants waited. Bowing very low, the clerk informed them that Mr. Darrin had returned and had gone to his apartment.

"The number of that apartment?" cried Toruma.

The clerk gave the number, forgetting to add that Mrs. Darrin was also there. Nor did the Japanese officers remember that Dave was married.

So, Toruma leading the way, the three filed up the stairs, sought the apartment, and knocked on the door.

Inside, Belle, the lacquer box in her hand, and supposing that it was a servant who had knocked, stepped over to open the door.

And there she stood in the doorway, the lacquer box in her hand, the medallion plainly showing.

The eyes of the three young officers immediately turned toward that priceless heirloom, not a betraying sign came to their faces.

"A thousand pardons, madam," begged Toruma. "We have knocked at the wrong door. We sought the apartment of Mr. Darrin."

"Then you have found the right door," smiled Belle. "I am Mrs. Darrin. Unfortunately, my husband is out."

"We were wrongly informed that he had returned," apologized Toruma, bowing low. "We crave a thousand pardons, and hasten to withdraw."

"Shall I tell Mr. Darrin who called?" asked Belle.

"We shall do ourselves the honor to see Mr. Darrin soon after he returns," replied Lieutenant Toruma sweetly, in a voice in which there was no suspicion of menace.

"Who asks for me, gentlemen?" hailed a merry voice, as Ensign Dave Darrin rounded a turn in the corridor, and came upon the party. "Toruma? Katura? Hata? This *is* a pleasure."

"We shall go to the main parlor below," said Toruma courteously, taking the hand that Dave extended, as did the others. "May we hope to see you there, sir, at your own convenience?"

"I will be down inside of five minutes," Dave promised lightly, and the Japanese bowed themselves away.

Unconsciously Belle had thrown behind her the hand that held the lacquer box. For that reason Dave did not see it until he had stepped inside and had closed the door after him.

Then, of a sudden, young Mrs. Darrin remembered her surprise, and held forward the box in such a way as to display the medallion lying in it.

"I have something strange, Dave dear, to tell you about this," she announced.

With an astonished cry Dave caught up the box.

"Why it is—it must be—the heirloom that Katura showed me at the American Club this morning," he uttered.

"Mr. Katura's?" echoed Belle.

"Yes. And so he came here and offered it to you? Belle, my dear, we cannot accept such—"

"Oh, do you think it could have been Mr. Katura who sent it to me?" the young wife asked.

"Sent it to you? Don't you know who gave it to you?" Ensign Darrin asked, in amazement. "Didn't he hand it to you just now?"

"Oh, no, indeed!" Belle exclaimed. "Listen, Dave."

Thereupon Mrs. Darrin related all she knew of the matter. She and Dave spent some minutes together in hunting for the strange note, which could not be found.

"No use in looking any further," Darrin declared, at last. "Besides Katura is waiting for me below. I will take this medallion back to him. Certainly he can clear up the matter for me."

Full of uprightness of purpose Dave Darrin started below, to face a storm that was certain to be past his comprehension.

CHAPTER XVIII—MR. KATURA DOES SOME ASTOUNDING

"Katura, my dear fellow, I'm immensely sorry to have kept you waiting," cried Dave genially, as he entered the parlor. His nod took in Toruma and Hata as well.

"The waiting has not been tiresome," replied Katura coldly, rising to his feet, as did his comrades in arms.

"And now, Katura," Dave went on, "I am going to ask you if you can clear up the mystery as to how this medallion, this magnificent heirloom of yours, fell into Mrs. Darrin's hands."

"I came to see if *you* could account for that," replied the little lieutenant coldly, though his face still wore a smile.

"Why, what do you mean?" asked Dave. "All I know is that, upon my return, I found that Mrs. Darrin had been presented, under very strange circumstances, with this medallion, which I instantly recognized as yours."

"I saw it in her hand when she opened the door to us," Katura answered. "Beyond that, about all that I know, Mr. Darrin, is that, upon my arrival at the Okugawa Bank, I found the box missing from the pocket in which I had placed it."

"Then it was not you who sent this box and its contents to Mrs. Darrin?" the American ensign demanded.

"I did not send it to her," Katura rejoined.

"Then how did she come to receive it?"

"That is what I have come to ask you, Mr. Darrin," returned the little infantry lieutenant.

"What do you mean?" asked Dave, coloring slightly, for, despite the smiles on the three Japanese faces, there was something accusing in their manners.

"How did this box happen to reach your wife?" asked Lieutenant Hata, gravely.

Dave frankly related the circumstances as told him by his wife.

"If we could see the note, that might throw some light on the matter," suggested Lieutenant Hata, darkly.

"That is the curious part of it, gentlemen," said Dave, gravely. "Soon after the gift came that note disappeared, and neither Mrs. Darrin nor I have been able to find any trace of it."

"That is certainly remarkable," said Hata, with emphasis.

"Very remarkable," agreed Toruma.

"So remarkable," added Katura, "that I cannot comprehend it at all."

"At any rate, before I leave Tokio," proposed Darrin, "I shall hope to have the whole matter cleared up."

For the second time Lieutenant Katura's face flushed a fiery red. He could not help feeling that he was being lightly or insolently used. In his own mind the Japanese was not prepared to suspect an American officer and gentleman of deliberate theft.

"Mr. Darrin," asked Katura, "is this your idea of a really clever joke?"

"What do you mean, sir?" demanded Dave Darrin, flushing in turn.

"Can you realize, sir, how I must have felt," the little lieutenant went on, "when my mother permitted me to take this medallion from the bank vault to show it to American friends, and then I returned to the bank to find that the heirloom was missing from my pocket?"

"I have told you all that I know about the matter," Ensign Dave insisted with dignity. "Is that not enough?"

"No, sir, it is not!" replied Lieutenant Katura, firmly. "I trust you will pardon me when I say that it was all a very stupid joke!"

"Joke?" gasped Dave. "Do you mean—"

He paused, unwilling to finish the sentence, for it seemed to him that this angry little Japanese had suddenly thrown a doubt around Mrs. Darrin's word.

"You have no further explanation to offer me?" asked Katura frigidly.

"There is no other explanation to be offered, sir," Dave Darrin returned, with equal stiffness.

"Then I am sorry, but I have to do—this!"

Advancing a step or two, Lieutenant Katura landed the flat of his right hand across the cheek of the American ensign.

Swifter than a flash Ensign Darrin returned the insult in the same manner.

"That is enough of this, between gentlemen," exclaimed Lieutenant Toruma, leaping between the two angry young officers. Hata followed, saying:

"Quite enough!"

"The rest," remarked Toruma, "can be settled in a much different fashion."

Dave cooled down a bit, realizing that he had sustained himself by returning the insult in the same form in which it had been delivered. Unless he were struck again he did not propose to discredit himself by brawling in the parlor of a hotel.

Katura, after a moment of sullenness, flashed at Toruma a look that the latter quite understood.

"Have you any idea, Mr. Darrin," Toruma asked, "when I shall be fortunate enough to find Mr. Dalzell in?"

"Probably at about five-thirty," Dave answered. "He will wish to dress, and we dine at six."

"Then we will do ourselves the honor of wishing you good afternoon," said Hata, bowing low. In another moment the three Japanese had left the room.

"Well, of all the odd experiences!" muttered Ensign Darrin, frowning. After a moment or two he left the parlor, going direct to his apartment.

"Was it Mr. Katura who sent me that medallion?" asked Belle, at once.

"He says not," Dave answered.

"Then who—"

"Belle, dear, do you mind letting me think this little puzzle out in silence?" begged Dave.

For a long time he sat silent. At last he told Belle what had happened below.

"But why should Mr. Katura strike you?" asked Belle, her eyes flashing.

"That is what I cannot understand," Dave rejoined, in a hurt tone. "I have looked upon Katura as a fine little fellow, and I imagine him to be the soul of honor."

"Does he doubt your word, then, about the manner in which the medallion came into our possession?" Belle quizzed.

"He had better not," her young husband retorted. "I would not be patient under an insinuation that my word is doubted. Belle, I cannot explain any single part of the matter."

So the pair talked it over for a long time, but no point in the tangle became a whit clearer.

Late in the afternoon there came a knock at the door.

"Come in," called Dave.

"Hullo! There you are," cried Danny Grin, opening the door a little and showing his head. "Good afternoon, Mrs. Darrin. Dave, old fellow, have you time to favor me with just a little visit in my room?"

"Why, certainly," assented Darrin, rising at once, for there was suppressed excitement in Dalzell's voice.

Dan, however, remained silent until he had led the way down the corridor and had closed the door of his room on the chums.

"Now, Dave," gasped the other young ensign, "what is all this about?"

"What is what about?" parried Dave.

"Why," Danny rattled on, "there is some yarn about Katura's medallion having come into your possession. You and Katura had some words in the parlor, and he struck you in the face."

"And I promptly returned the blow in kind," Darrin responded.

"Exactly," nodded Dalzell. "That appears to have been the start that is to lead up to something very pretty. When I came in I found Toruma and Hata awaiting me. They told me that Katura had sent them to see me, or any other friend or friends who you may prefer, to arrange for a meeting at which the memory of the blows exchanged should be wiped out. In plain words, David, little giant, you are challenged to fight a duel with Lieutenant Katura."

"A duel?" echoed Dave Darrin, aghast. "That's a joke!"

"If it is," retorted Danny Grin, dryly, "then please help me to find out the point at which I am to laugh."

"But I have sworn to uphold the laws of the United States and to obey the regulations of the United States Navy," Dave continued, "and dueling is against the regulations."

"It looks," returned Dan, soberly, "as though you would have to fight, or 'lose face.'"

"And if I engage in a duel," Dave retorted, "I have perjured myself, for I shall have broken the regulations that I am sworn to obey."

"Well, then," Dan inquired, "what *are* you going to do? Go back aboard the 'Katahdin' and forego all shore leave as long as we are in Japanese waters? But, for that matter, would naval officers of any foreign service respect you anywhere in the world? For the officers of most navies still fight duels at need, and the Japanese officers would be likely to snub you, in every foreign port, for what they would consider your 'shame.'"

"But on what basis am I expected to fight?" Dave demanded. "Because I answered Katura's blow on the face?"

"I suppose that is the pretended reason," Dalzell answered, gravely. "Of course every one familiar with dueling will know that some deeper cause exists."

"It must be the inexplicable matter of the medallion that makes Katura so anxious to slit my windpipe with a sword, or drive a bullet through my breast," Dave went on. "I must tell you, Dan, all that I know about this wretched matter of the medallion."

Danny Grin's eyes opened wider and wider as he heard the tale.

"That's the story," nodded Dalzell vigorously, when he had heard it all. "I understand now. Katura can't think that you *stole* the medallion. That would be altogether contrary to the nature of an officer and a gentleman. But he figures that you took the medallion from him as a joke, and when he realizes that you, in turn, might have lost it, and thinks of the anguish of his mother, who owns the medallion, then Katura's blood is up, and he must fight you. Hence, he gave you the blow in the face, which you returned. Therefore, according to the ideals of the duello, you owe him a meeting on the field of honor."

"That field of honor will have grown into a forest, if he waits until I meet him there," Dave declared firmly.

"Then you simply won't fight a duel."

"I shall not!"

"What grounds shall I give for your refusal?"

"Simply tell Katura's seconds that duelling is against the United States Naval Regulations, which I have sworn to obey and uphold. Tell Mr. Katura's seconds that I decline, on any pretext, to break the regulations knowingly."

"Whew!" whistled Danny Grin. "The Japanese smile is historic, and a thing of beauty, but I can see the assortment of Japanese smiles that will greet any such reply on my part. I shall get a regular Japanese horse laugh!"

"Then when you meet Toruma and Hata, cut the interview as short as you can," Dave suggested, "and get it over with. But make it as plain as you know how that I simply won't fight a duel."

"Oh, I can make it plain enough, and they will believe me in a minute—no trouble about that," Dan murmured as he rose. "But they will decline to believe in your lofty ideas of right and wrong, and will set it all down to plain American cowardice."

"I am sorry to impose any such errand upon you, Danny boy," sighed Dave. "But I will go with you, and speak for myself."

"Oh, that wouldn't do at all," protested Dan, aghast. "In dueling the principal never goes to meet the other chap's seconds. His own second must do that for him."

"But there isn't going to be any duel," smiled Dave, "and I am not a principal, nor are you my second. You are my friend, and the best in the world, but you will never be my second."

"There's going to be the dickens of a mix-up," grunted Dalzell, as, after wringing Darrin's hand, he moved toward the door. "I'll do the best I can, but you must expect, after declining a duel, to be snubbed everywhere in Tokio."

"Then I shall endeavor to set Tokio an example in calmness," smiled Dave again. But the instant that the door had closed on him, and he strolled down the hallway, a thoughtful frown came to his face.

In the meantime Dan Dalzell was hastening below, on a by no means pleasant mission.

Just now Dave did not want to go back to Belle, for fear she might question him. After a turn or two he went back to Dalzell's room.

Half an hour later, growing impatient, Dave decided to go below and to address Toruma and Hata himself.

Down in the lobby Ensign Dave beheld Lieutenants Toruma and Hata, talking with two men who looked like Englishmen.

"Dan must have finished his part," thought Dave. "I'll see if I can draw Toruma aside."

Just as Dave Darrin approached the group Toruma caught sight of him.

Some low-voiced remark ran through the group.

"May I have a word with you, Mr. Toruma, at your convenience?" Dave inquired.

There was no reply. The two Japanese and the English pair merely wheeled about abruptly, turning their backs upon him.

CHAPTER XIX—DAN FIRES A WARM SHOT

Flushing slightly, though with no other outward sign, Dave turned upon his heel and left the group.

"I can understand the attitude of the Japanese officers, but why should Englishmen turn against me?" Dave wondered. "The average Englishman has no more patience with silly dueling than we Americans have."

It would have done Dave's heart good, just then, had he known how Danny Grin had met and talked to the two Japanese seconds.

On hearing that Ensign Darrin would not, under any circumstances, consent to a duel, Toruma and Hata had smiled as genially as Dan had expected they would do.

"I don't know," pursued Dan, "whether you can understand the feelings that prompt an officer to decline a duel."

"The reason that comes most quickly to mind," replied Toruma, "is the feeling of fear."

"Gentlemen, if you think that my friend, Darrin, is afraid of anything that is honorable, then you are poor judges of human nature," Dan replied, with some warmth.

"But why should a naval man hesitate to accept the appeal to arms?" inquired Toruma, with another smile.

"Darrin, to my positive knowledge, never did meet any call to arms with anything except calm joy," Dalzell replied warmly. "In this present instance, if one of Mr. Darrin's superior officers gave him an order to meet Mr. Katura on the field of honor, Darrin would be there ahead of time. But Mr. Darrin took the oath of the service, binding him to obey the Navy regulations, and one of those regulations expressly forbids him to fight duels, or to take any part in one."

"What shall we tell Mr. Katura?" pressed Hata darkly.

"Tell him anything you please," offered Danny Grin obligingly.

"But he will feel at once, as we do, that Mr. Darrin declines the meeting because Mr. Darrin has not the valor to meet a resolute man on the field of honor."

Danny Grin looked thoughtful for a minute. Then he glanced up to ask:

"How much actual military service, under fire, have you seen, Mr. Toruma?"

"It has not, as yet, been my good fortune to see any," replied Lieutenant Toruma.

"And you, Mr. Hata, may I inquire what is the extent of your service?"

"I have been as unfortunate in that respect as my friend, Toruma," replied Hata.

"Mr. Katura must have seen some active, hard service," pressed Danny Grin.

"Alas, no," Toruma answered, "Mr. Katura has not been any more fortunate than have we."

"Darrin has seen some service," Danny Grin went on calmly. "He was commended in orders for gallant and daring work when the Navy took Vera Cruz. Then, down in Vengara, in South America, in a revolution, he went, with one companion, into the wilds of Vengara to visit the camp of the former dictator, Benedito, who had an army behind him, fighting the government of Vengara. With the help of only that one companion, Darrin, in the heart of Benedito's own army, took the ex-dictator captive, at the point of a revolver, and brought him through the forests, through the government lines as well, and turned General Benedito over to the United States forces."

"That was a splendid deed," bowed Toruma.

"Have you heard of the recent conduct of our Navy at Nu-ping, China?" Dan asked.

"Oh, yes," nodded Toruma. "That was an excellently managed affair, and one highly creditable to your Navy."

"The officer who was in command at Nu-ping," continued Dalzell, "was David Darrin, Ensign, United States Navy."

"He did a splendid act," admitted Lieutenant Toruma, bowing.

"And now," added Lieutenant Hata, "he impresses others as being afraid to meet a gentleman on the field of honor!"

"When a man has such a record, don't officers like you and Mr. Katura, who have never smelled burning powder, feel like boys criticizing the courage of a veteran?" asked Dan dryly. With the words, Dan, with one of his famous and sardonic grins, turned on his heel and walked away, leaving the two very much ruffled young Japanese officers.

Dave Darrin, after his rebuff in the lobby, stepped slowly toward the door.

"I'll go outside for a while before I go back to Belle," he decided.

Within five minutes he ran into Dalzell, who at once told him of the interview with the two Japanese.

"The end is not yet," sighed Dave. "But now suppose we return and dress for dinner. Remember, no word of this to Belle. I don't want her vacation spoiled if I can help it."

But could he help it? Apparently no one at the tables noticed Belle and the two young ensigns as they made their way through the dining room.

"Did you notice, Dave, that none of the Japanese officers, and there were a good many of them in the room, rose and bowed to me tonight? What can the matter be?"

"Let us hope," answered Dave, "they're absorbed in their own affairs."

Belle noted, however, that throughout the meal and on their leaving the room, no one except some United States naval officers and two American infantry officers on leave offered them the slightest courtesy.

Leaving Belle in the parlor, the two young officers returned to the lobby. They were shortly approached by Lieutenant Commander Emery of the "Katahdin."

"Hullo, Darrin. Evening, Dalzell. Now Darrin, what is this rumor about your refusing to meet a Japanese officer on the field?" he asked abruptly.

"There was a challenge, yes," admitted Dave. "I declined on the ground that our regulations forbid dueling."

"Of course you couldn't fight," responded the lieutenant commander. "But hadn't you better go back to the ship and remain there as long as she lies in Yokohama?"

"And give up my vacation with Belle?"

"Don't you realize what it means in some countries to decline a duel, Darrin? You'll be an outcast in Tokio. For Mrs. Darrin's sake, don't remain ashore and let her be tormented by the studied coldness that will be shown you everywhere in Tokio."

"They may think me a coward for not fighting, but I can't be coward enough to run from the consequences, though I dislike to involve Belle in this."

"Here comes Decoeur of the French Navy," said Lieutenant Commander Emery suddenly. "I want to shake hands with him."

Decoeur, looking slightly embarrassed, shook hands very cordially with Emery, who then rather abruptly introduced his brother officers, Mr. Darrin and Mr. Dalzell.

The French officer gave the ensigns only the shadow of a bow. His hand did not come forward. Then he passed stiffly on.

"You see," said Emery. "You understand what the attitude in Tokio will be. Are you going to subject Mrs. Darrin to such humiliations?"

"I don't see how I can avoid it," replied Dave, sick at heart on Belle's account.

CHAPTER XX—CONCLUSION

"Isn't this delightful?" cried Belle, holding up a card that she had received in the mail that morning. "Mrs. Fullerton of the Embassy has secured for us this invitation to the reception that the Prime Minister of Japan gives to the Emperor this afternoon at the Prime Minister's official residence."

"There'll be a dreadful crush there," replied Dave, with a secret sinking at heart.

"Of course, if you don't care to go—" began Belle considerately.

"Of course I want to go," Dave returned bravely. "Do you think we'd miss such an event as this will certainly be?"

"Going to the reception this afternoon?" asked Dan a little later.

"Certainly; Belle has a card for us."

"And yet Toruma and Hata say that you have no courage!"

"Are you invited?" Dave asked.

"Oh, yes. And going, of course."

Three o'clock that afternoon the young people entered the carriage that Dave had ordered. The drive to the Prime Minister's residence was not long, but it took time to get through the crush of carriages that filled the last two blocks. Even after the carriage had delivered its passengers at the door, it was another long time before the Darrin party succeeded in making its way through the throng to the hall in which the reception was being held.

As yet their Majesties had not arrived. The Prime Minister and his wife were receiving guests. Their Majesties would arrive late and depart not long afterwards.

The names of Ensign and Mrs. Darrin and Ensign Dalzell, United States Navy, were called at the door. Only those nearest the entrance could hear the names announced. But at the mention of theirs, Dave could see many an epauleted shoulder turn aside so as not to see the Darrin party.

In due time they made their bows to Prime Minister Kotito and his wife. Then they were swept to the far end of the room. Presently Lieutenant Commander Emery came to them.

"Darrin," he said, after greeting Belle, "word has come that their Majesties are on their way. According to custom, the officers of whatever service or country who may be present are going out. In the street, they will take places on the outer edge of the throng and salute the Emperor and the Empress. I'll take Mrs. Darrin to the Embassy party, then return and go outside with you."

"You are very kind," replied Dave, and Belle, accepting Emery's arm, was led away.

Emery was back quickly, but just outside the house he was accidentally separated from the two ensigns.

"Suppose we go farther up the street, Dave," suggested Dan. "I'd like to be in the very first squad to salute their Majesties."

So past the uniformed groups and through the crowd the two made their way. When they halted they were about fifty feet beyond the nearest group of uniformed men.

The procession came into sight. Just before the imperial carriage reached the spot where they stood, both ensigns brought up their hands in a military salute. Then, so rapidly that it seemed part of the same movement, they raised their caps in homage to the Empress.

The Emperor beheld the salute and bent his head in acknowledgment of the tribute.

Spt! Spt! Sizz-zz!

Dave Darrin's military training made him start at the sound. Taller by a head than the Japanese in front of him, Dave's eye caught sight of something that escaped the other onlookers.

"Quick, Dan!" he shouted. "A leg up!"

Though Dalzell did not know what the trouble was, he seized Dave below the hips, raising him as though to boost him over a high wall.

Over the heads of those in front of him plunged Dave Darrin. He came down, grappling with a sullen-looking Japanese, who, crouching over, held something concealed.

Spt! Sizz-zz!

Dave grappled with the man, who was trying to conceal the sputtering bomb preparatory to throwing it. Down in a heap went Dave and the Japanese, the sizzing bomb under both.

Standing close to the scoundrel with the bomb, were three other political malcontents, and these men now let knives slip down from their sleeves and sprang at the young ensign.

By this time Dan had reached his friend's side and, using his fist, struck down the fellow who was nearest to Dave.

Frightened screams arose on the air as word flew through the crowd.

Police heard, and, understanding, charged through the crowd. Soldiers heard, and used their clubbed rifles in an effort to get through to the scene of disorder.

Meanwhile, Dave Darrin was fighting with the man underneath him—the man who held the bomb that was about to explode. Suddenly Dave leaped up, leaving his opponent unconscious. In the half-second before getting to his feet, Darrin had taken the sputtering, glowing fuse between finger and thumb. Though his hand was being burned and blistered, he held on until he knew that the danger was past.

"Throw it away from their Majesties' carriage," implored the Japanese who could speak English.

"No need to now!" called Dave steadily, holding up the bomb to show the fuse was out.

In these few pulsing moments the speed of the Emperor's carriage had not been increased. Neither the ruler nor his consort looked about.

The crowd was wild, and would have torn the miscreants to pieces, but the police blocked the attempt, and the men were marched away.

Dave and Dan were trying to hide themselves by mingling with the crowd, but a Japanese army officer, a general of division, hurried up to them, followed by members of his staff.

"Pardon, gentlemen, you must not go yet. You have done Japan a great service. The Government must know the names of such brave officers."

Though reluctant to do so, the ensigns were forced by courtesy to give their names to General Kagi, as he introduced himself. Through the crowd, silent through respect for the Americans and thankfulness for the safety of their sovereigns, the general led the way to the residence of the Prime Minister. There was a conversation with a high official, then General Kagi said:

"Gentlemen, since this is a public reception, their Majesties wish to thank you in public for your heroic conduct this day."

"It will be very embarrassing, General," Dave answered, smiling but hesitant.

Having traversed a long corridor and several rooms, Dave and Dan looked through a door that was opened to them to a dais where the imperial pair stood under a canopy.

At sight of General Kagi and the youths, several resplendent officials came forward, and Darrin and Dalzell were conducted to this dais. At a signal, Dave and Dan made a low bow.

First the Emperor thanked the young officers for what they had done, speaking in Japanese and having it immediately repeated in English. Then her Majesty said a few words.

"You may reply," whispered an official.

Making another low bow, Darrin answered:

"I am grateful to have been permitted to render some service to their Majesties, the Emperor and the Empress of Japan."

Dan's face, at first fiery red, went pale as he in turn made another low bow. He could think of nothing to say. His mind seemed blank. He felt he was going to make a fool of himself. But his head was now as low as he could make it, and he knew he must say something. Then, his voice sounding as though some one across the room were speaking, Dan heard himself say:

"Mine were but a pair of hands to assist my comrade. Neither of us was moved from within in the little that we were able to do. We were but the tools of Providence, which could not see the virtues of their Majesties perish."

Though all Japanese eyes were downcast, there was a flash of gratitude in every pair as Dan's speech was put into Japanese; though Dan himself could never be made to understand what a tactful one it was.

Dave and Dan having followed their conductors to the right of the dais, his Majesty spoke briefly for the Empress and himself, the words being translated into English and French for the benefit of the divers nationalities represented. Their Majesties then withdrew and the reception was soon over, though Dave and Dan found themselves embarrassed frequently during the next few days by impromptu receptions in all sorts of places—shops, streets, the hotel lobby—by grateful and admiring crowds.

It was on the day following the reception at the Prime Minister's residence that Dave received a note. Belle and Dan were present when he got it, and, apologizing, he broke the seal. Then he read aloud the brief note from Katura.

"'That I did you a deep wrong I am convinced. I shall not crave your pardon until I am able to do more. I trust you will not leave Tokio before I have the honor of seeing you. All I can now say is that I am investigating.'"

"What does he mean?" asked Belle wonderingly. "I have of course known something was wrong, for I could see that we were avoided; but I knew you were trying to keep it from me, so did not ask questions. But——"

"Yes, you had better know the whole story. Perhaps I should have told you at first," replied Dave. So he told her all, not without help from Dan, who thought Dave too modest.

Dave wanted to get out of Tokio and away from the unwelcome publicity. But Belle persuaded him to await Katura's explanation. It came within three or four days.

Toruma called at the hotel. Dave met him with cordiality, then the Japanese said:

"I have come on account of my friend, Mr. Katura. Mr. Katura's regrettable challenge grew out of the affair of the medallion."

"Under the circumstances," said Dave, "I can not blame him for suspecting me of stealing it."

"Not stealing it! He thought it an inconsiderate joke! An American told us that he had seen you slip your hand into Katura's pocket and take out a lacquer box. That box belongs to Katura's mother and is very precious to her."

"An American?"

"Yes; Simmons. But he was working for a man, English or American, named Pembroke."

Then Dave understood. Pembroke, angered by the humiliation at the yamen and more so because he himself had confessed when he thought he was about to die, had hired this man to help him in his scheme of vengeance.

"This Simmons is a criminal and has keys that open many doors, so, after delivering the package to Mrs. Darrin, he later entered the room and secured the note that had gone with the box."

"Why did they not sell the medallion?"

"That would have been impossible. It is too well known here for anyone to handle it safely."

Katura called and tried to apologize, something that Dave Darrin would not allow. He asked Katura and Toruma and Hata to dinner to meet Belle, and the officers parted as friends.

It was a year later that Dave and Dan heard that Bishop Whitlock and his missionaries had gone back to Nu-ping and that a new governor had been appointed for the province. They learned, too, that "Burnt-face" was dead of cholera and that Miss Chapin was married to her missionary lover.

The ensigns' leave was up, and, parting regretfully with Belle, they returned to their ship. There they found new honors awaiting them. On their arrival the Admiral sent for them and read them a despatch, signed by the Secretary of the Navy.

"'The President directs that you extend to Ensigns Darrin and Dalzell his thanks and commendation for their conduct in preventing the assault on the Emperor and Empress of Japan. At appropriate time you will publicly commend these officers.'"

They learned too that as soon as they expressed their willingness to accept the honor they would be commissioned as lieutenants, junior grade.

"Accept! You bet we'll accept!" said Dan, but not in those words before the Admiral.

One other honor was to come to them. The Emperor bestowed on them the decoration, second class, of the Order of the Rising Sun, a decoration that Congress allowed them to accept.

But now Dave's ship sailed away under sealed orders, leaving Belle to wonder when she would again see her husband. When this time was and where, will be told in another volume: "Dave Darrin and the German Submarines; or Making a Clean-up of the Hun Sea Monsters."

THE END

CPSIA information can be obtained at www.ICGtesting.com
Printed in the USA
LVOW01s1641240114

370878LV00035B/1165/P